The Highland valleys of New Guinea are the
setting for this towering, dramatic novel by
Morris L West. In an atmosphere of
brooding suspense the actors play their parts:
Kumo, the sorcerer; N'Daria, the sensual
native girl who shares the world of white
man and black; the doctor's wife Gerda and
the men who love her. To the thundering beat of
the kundu drums the story drives with
ever quickening pulse to an explosive climax.

Also by Morris L West

Morris L West

Kundu

MAYFLOWER
GRANADA PUBLISHING
London Toronto Sydney New York

Published by Granada Publishing Limited
in Mayflower Books 1965
Reprinted 1965, 1968, 1970, 1973, 1978

ISBN 0 583 113028 3

First published in Great Britain by
Angus and Robertson Ltd
Copyright © Morris L West

Granada Publishing Limited
Frogmore, St Albans, Herts AL2 2NF
and
3 Upper James Street, London W1R 4BP
1221 Avenue of the Americas, New York, NY10020, USA
117 York Street, Sydney, NSW 2000, Australia
100 Skyway Avenue, Toronto, Ontario, Canada M9W 3A6
Trio City, Coventry Street, Johannesburg 2001, South Africa
CML Centre, Queen & Wyndham, Auckland 1, New Zealand

Made and printed in Great Britain by
C. Nicholls & Company Ltd
The Philips Park Press, Manchester
Set in Linotype Caledonia

*For Des and Edna who introduced us to
the Fabulous Island*

AUTHOR'S NOTE

This is a work of fiction. The background is a composite. The manners and customs are borrowed from many places in New Guinea and Papua. If the characters seem to resemble any person living or dead, it is by accident, which no writer can avoid. Many of the incidents have their basis in fact and the conflicts here heightened and given dramatic form are implicit in the latest and boldest colonial experiment, the Trustee Administration of New Guinea.

M.L.W.

CHAPTER 1

IT was four in the afternoon. The sun was westering along the green valley. The first streamers of cloud were creeping along the northern barrier, whose peaks heaved themselves up, cobalt against the peach tints of the sky.

It was still summer in Capricorn. Down on the coast, in Lae and Madang and Wewak, they sweltered and swore and whistled for the cool, night winds. Up here, in the Highland valleys, five thousand feet above the sea, the warmth was waning, and, when darkness came, it would be cold.

On the broad stoop of his bungalow, thatched with Nipa palm and framed with bamboo, Kurt Sonderfeld stood looking out across the valley where the young coffee was growing under the rows of shade-trees, towards the huts of the Chimbu village and the formal avenue of the dancing park.

He was restless, though few would have guessed it. The quality of containment, which was so much of his nature, the capacity for control, so long and painfully developed, were armour enough against betrayal.

But even had they guessed, they would have been hard put to name a cause. He had a wife whose brooding Slavic beauty was a legend from Madang to Mount Hagen. His coffee was healthy. His past was safely buried. The Administration approved him. He was master in his own valley, fifty miles from the scrutiny of the District Commissioner at Goroka.

Yet he was restless. His fine cigar tasted sour. He found no pleasure in the prospect that began with the green lawns of his bungalow and swept away to the foot of the purple mountains, whose brown people served him as they served few other white men, with awe and with alacrity.

7

Tonight, of all nights, he needed privacy. Tonight, of all nights, it would be denied to him. Within an hour his guests would arrive. They would sit on his veranda and drink his whisky and eat his food and talk, volubly, emphatically, as lonely men do, far into the darkness, while the kundus throbbed and the chants of the villagers drifted up on the breeze.

Zum Teufel! Let them come!

He tossed his cigar away and watched it smoulder on the black earth of the garden.

He was a tall man, broad-barrelled, square-shouldered, straight as a pine-tree. His deep forehead rose, dome-like, to the line of his red, cropped hair, and a brown scar ran clean along the line of his jaw from the earlobe to the cleft of his blunt chin. His mouth was tight as a trap.

For a long moment he stood there, moving his hand along the shining bamboo rail as if smoothing out his own ruffled temper. Then his mouth relaxed and he stepped off the veranda and strode down the gravelled path towards a small bamboo hut on the fringe of the plantation.

This was his laboratory, compact and efficient as he was himself. Here, he was no longer Kurt Sonderfeld, migrant by necessity, medico by grace and favour, lessee planter under the Trustee Administration. Here he was Kurt Sonderfeld, Doctor of Medicine – Freiburg and Bonn, Honorary Adviser on Malarial Control in the Eastern Highlands, contributor to learned journals, correspondent of learned societies in Europe and the United States. He grinned sourly as the ripples stirred in the pools of memory. So many of his colleagues had found their past a handicap in a new country. Kurt Sonderfeld had turned his own dubious history to handsome profit.

He pushed open the door of the hut and walked in.

There was a girl sitting at the long bench under the window. She had a microscope in front of her and a

8

pad of notes at her elbow. As Sonderfeld entered, she looked up and her mouth parted in a wide grin.

She had a broad nose and the full, thrusting lips of the mountain people. Her skin was brown as bush honey and her hair was crisped in tight ringlets close to her skull. Yet she was beautiful – beautiful with youth and health. Her skin glowed warmly and her round breasts were firm and challenging under the gaudy, pink, print dress.

Sonderfeld towered over her, smiling in cynical approval.

"Well? What do you find, N'Daria?"

His voice was deep, and one had to listen carefully to catch the tell-tale intonation of the Continental.

She answered him in mission English, husky and precise.

"These are the eggs we took from the lower pond."

"Yes?"

"Anopheles."

Sonderfeld nodded.

"I expected it."

"So now we have the fever in the valley?"

"Not yet. But when the boys come back from the coast they will bring the fever with them. These fellows –"

He tapped the barrel of the microscope. "These fellows will carry it to the rest of the tribe."

The girl said nothing. She was watching him, lips parted, eyes wide, head tilted back, so that he could see the hollow of her throat and the slow downward curving of her breasts.

Sonderfeld watched her with satisfaction and amusement. This was his own creation. This he had wrought meticulously, patiently, as a man might make a delicate instrument, calculating each movement and function, balancing it against the next until he could say with mathematical certainty: "This is mine. Use it so . . . and it will work thus and thus."

She had come from Père Louis' Mission School as

9

househelp to Gerda. But with N'Daria the veneer of the Mission was thin and cracked before it was fully dry. Underneath was the primitive, full of the old fears, the old superstitions, the old violent passions. But he had tamed her – tamed her with subtlety and severity and rare gentleness. And as he tamed, he taught, so that she could work with him accurately, scrupulously, as he worked himself.

Now she was ready. But the work he had in mind for her was ten thousand years away from the bright instruments of the laboratory.

Still smiling, he laid the tip of his finger on her neck, pressing it gently into the hollow behind the ear. She shivered at his touch, but did not draw away. Slowly, deliberately, he drew his finger down and across her throat so that his nail raised a thin weal under the honey-coloured skin. She trembled. Moisture formed at the corners of her mouth and split on her dark lips. Her eyes were flecked and lit with sudden desire.

"Do you care?" said Sonderfeld softly. "Do you care if the whole village dies of the fever?"

Her answer was a throaty whisper.

"No."

"Do you care if Kumo dies?"

"No."

"Good."

He withdrew his hand and she bent forward as if to renew the touch. Her whole body was alive with passion.

Sonderfeld grinned and shook his head.

"Not now, N'Daria."

"Tomorrow?"

"Perhaps . . . if you do well tonight. Get dressed now. Then come and show yourself to me."

Submissive, but heavy with dissatisfaction, she got up and walked to the screen door at the end of the hut. Sonderfeld watched her go and when the door closed behind her, he chuckled and bent over the microscope.

The small nodules of the mosquito larvae were monstrous under the powerful lens. N'Daria was right. They were anopheles, carrier of malaria. Now that the valley was open to traffic from Goroka and from the coast, it would be immune no longer. The pack-boys coming over the mountains would bring the disease; the patrol officers and the police-boys, the research men from the Department of Agriculture. Then it would break out in the villages and the children would sicken and die, and those who survived would have swollen spleens as big as pineapples, like the pitiful scarecrows on the Sepik Delta — unless Kurt Sonderfeld did something about it.

He would do it, of course, because order was necessary to his nature and to his plans. And because disease was a disorder, repugnant to him, he would stamp it out — tomorrow.

Tonight there were other matters. Tonight, if N'Daria did her part, the kundus would thunder the march of the conqueror and the chant would ring like a paean of victory. For a long time he sat, absorbed in his own thoughts, then the door creaked and he turned sharply.

N'Daria was standing before him.

Bark cloth was wound about her loins and her pubic apron was of dyed and plaited grass. From navel to diaphragm, her belly was bound with a belt of plaited cane. Her up-thrust breasts were bare, and ropes of red and blue beads hung down in the hollow between them. Her septum was pierced with a curved sliver of pearl-shell and her fuzzy head was crowned with a casque of iridescent beetles, surmounted by the scarlet feathers of the Bird of Paradise. Her naked skin was shiny with tree oil. . . .

Sonderfeld stared at her with admiration. He felt the slow, dangerous itch creep into his loins. He fought against it, angrily. The girl was his to take at any time — but not tonight. He saw her grin at his discomfort and cursed himself for a fool.

"Come here, N'Daria!"

11

She came to him, slowly, rolling her hips. She stood before him, head tilted back, and he smelt the oil and the heat of her body.

Perhaps, in spite of himself, the big man would take her now. Again, she was disappointed.

Her eyes pleaded with him. He laughed at her frustration.

"Tomorrow, N'Daria – tomorrow. Now, show me !"

She plunged her fingers between the broad cane belt and her skin, and brought out a small tampon of cotton-wool.

"Good. Put it back !"

She replaced the cottonwool and waited, slack and submissive.

"Now tell me."

"Tonight I am to bring you –"

"No. Tell me from the beginning."

She took a deep breath and began again, her husky voice piecing out the directions slowly in the alien tongue.

"Tonight, in the village, the unmarried ones make kunande. We sit and sing and roll our faces together. Kumo will be there and we will make kunande together. Then we will go to my sister's house. We will eat and drink and Kumo and I will carry-leg. He will play with me and I will play with him. Then, when he is full of desire, we will go into the bushes and he will take me."

"Can you be sure of that?"

Her plumed head went up proudly.

"I am sure. Kumo desires me. I always please him."

"See that you please him tonight. What then?"

"When he takes me . . ." said N'Daria with slow relish, ". . . when he takes me, he make spittle on my mouth. I will draw blood from his breast and from his shoulders. . . . Then, he will leave me."

"And when he leaves you?"

"I will come back to you and I will bring with me

the blood and the spittle and the seed of Kumo – and you will hold his life in your hands."

"So!" The word came out, a long, sighing breath of relief. The tension in him relaxed. His irritation drained away and power flowed back to him in long, smooth waves. He laid his hand on the brown shoulder and stroked it gently, caressingly.

"What you do for me tonight, N'Daria, you do for yourself. Remember that."

"I remember. And tomorrow . . . ?"

He smiled and brushed her breast with his finger-tips.

"Tomorrow, N'Daria, as you say. Go, now."

She was half-way to the door when he called her back.

"Tonight, when you return, I shall be at the house with the visitors. Light the lamp and hang it near the window. I will see it and will come when I can."

He took her to the door and stood watching her as she walked down the track to the village. She was like a bird, he thought, a small bright bird, with scarlet feathers, fluttering under the tangket-trees.

He closed the door of the laboratory and walked swiftly, purposefully, back to the house.

The canvas chairs were set on the stoop. There were glasses and a bucket of ice and jugs of frosted rain-water on the cane table and Wee Georgie, with tender care, was cutting the seal of a new bottle of Scotch.

He looked up as Sonderfeld mounted the steps, and his bloated face was distorted into a smile that displayed his gapped and rotten teeth. His voice was a piping cockney, incongruous in so large a man.

" 'Arf a minute, boss, and we're all set for the party. Care for a pipe-opener?"

"In a moment."

Sonderfeld surveyed him with weary distaste. Wee Georgie was one of his less successful enterprises. He was a head shorter than Sonderfeld, but his stumpy body was monstrous. His tousled head was set on two rolls of

13

blubber, his breasts were pendulous as a woman's and his belly was an obscene barrel scarcely covered by his shirt. His trouser-belt slipped under it like string round a rubber ball. His bow legs were knotted with blue veins and discoloured by ulcer scars. His misshapen feet were thrust into canvas shoes slit at both sides for comfort. When he laughed, which was often, he quaked like a jelly and his eyes were lost in the folds of his purple face. When he moved – which was as little as possible – he wheezed like a broken-winded nag.

"For God's sake, man, why don't you tidy your hair?" snapped Sonderfeld.

"I try, boss. Strike me dead, if I don't. Me girl tries, too, but it won't lie down. Not unless I douse it with oil. And you wouldn't want me stinking of pig fat while I serve the drinks. Now would you? Besides, me shirt's clean, isn't it – and me pants?"

"We should be thankful for so little, I suppose. Pour me a drink. A strong one."

He sat down in the nearest chair and watched Wee Georgie with sardonic amusement. The fellow's hands were trembling. He moistened his lips continually as he sniffed the liquor. It was one of Sonderfeld's small pleasures to calculate how long it would be before Wee Georgie would ask for a drink.

Wee Georgie was a survival from the pre-history of the Territory. His origins were misted with legend. He had been deck-hand on the copra-luggers, prospector, recruiter, waterfront pimp, and dozen other things, mercifully buried when the Japanese destroyed the records. Sonderfeld had picked him off the beach in Lae, cured him of clap, stones in the kidney, and a score of minor ailments, and brought him up to the valley as foreman to the boy labour and contact man with the tribes. He had settled down in squalid comfort with a pair of village girls and Sonderfeld thought he would die in twelve months of cirrhosis of the liver.

But by some miracle he managed to survive, and

Sonderfeld had made much profit from his alcoholic Caliban. Wee Georgie was a slovenly old reprobate, but he "thought kanaka" and he had no scruples. With care and caution and a judicious ration of liquor, he, too, had served the master-plan.

"There's your drink, boss."

"Thanks."

"Er – Ah – What about a small one for the help – eh, boss?"

Sonderfeld grinned and looked at his watch.

"Thirty seconds! You're doing well, my friend. You may have a drink."

"Thanks, boss – thanks."

He wheezed and chuckled and shuffled to the table to pour a stiff noggin.

"Mud in yer eye and pretty girls in yer bed!"

"*Prosit!*" said Kurt Sonderfeld absently.

Wee Georgie tossed his drink off with a practised gulp. His master drank slowly, savouring the spirit, feeling the slow warmth gather like warm coals in his belly. Drinking, for Sonderfeld, was a princely pleasure and he took it like a prince, with leisure and deliberation.

"Lansing's arrived, boss."

"Mr. Lansing to you, Georgie."

"Mr. Lansing, then. He came about half an hour ago."

"Where is he now?"

Sonderfeld put the question with studious indifference; but Wee Georgie's little eyes were lit with malicious humour.

"Out back. Looking at the flowers with Mrs. Sonderfeld."

"The poor fellow has few pleasures," said Sonderfeld, smoothly. "Who are we to deny him this one?"

Wee Georgie spat contemptuously over the railing.

"Few pleasures is right! What does he *do* down there in the village? Lives like a kanaka, he does. Eats their

15

food. Sits round the cook-fires. Never even touches the girls. What's the point in that, for Gawd's sake?"

"He's an anthropologist."

"Yup, I know. But what does he *do*?"

Sonderfeld stared into the golden liquor. His tone was velvet.

"He studies, Georgie. He studies the language, the beliefs, the manners, the customs, and the mating habits of the indigenous population. He is paid, I understand, by grant from an American foundation which finances such worthy enterprises."

"Paid? For what? Gawstrewth! I could tell 'em twice as much as Lansing'll ever know – and for half the price."

"I know. I know," said Sonderfeld gently. "But Lansing leaves out the dirty words."

"You're not very fond of Lansing, are you, boss?"

The whisky caught him full in the face. As he gasped and whimpered and rubbed his eyes, Sonderfeld jerked him upright by the hair and smacked him, full on the mouth. Then he chided him gently, without anger, as one admonishes a child.

"You will remember, Georgie, that you are a servant in this house. You will attend to my guests and mind your own business. You will remember that you are filth – alive by my skill and favour. You will have no more to drink this evening. Now clean yourself up and pour me a drink. Père Louis will be here any minute."

Wee Georgie backed away, a cowed, repulsive animal. Sonderfeld wiped his hands on a silk handkerchief and waited calmly for the arrival of his second guest.

The little priest came hurrying up the path, arms flailing, square beard bobbing on his chest. A small canvas bag hung over his shoulder and slapped up and down on his rump. His wizened, walnut face streamed with perspiration. He was like a goat, thought Sonderfeld, a wise and ancient goat with his grey beard and his bright, canny eyes. And yet of all the men who came to share his table, this was the one for whom he had most

16

respect. He must have been more than sixty, yet he had the gnarled and stringy strength of an old tree. More than thirty years of his life had been spent in the mountains of Papua and New Guinea. When the first prospectors came through the southern valley, Père Louis was there waiting for them. When the recruiters came in to the Highlands to find new labour pools, Père Louis was there to see that they kept their hands off his girls.

The years had not robbed him of his spry, peasant humour and, for all the isolation of his life, he was as modern a European as Sonderfeld had ever known. When they met, they spoke French first and then German. They talked books and medicine and politics and morals and philosophy; and when they parted Sonderfeld had the uneasy feeling that the little man had been sounding him, tapping the hollow places of his soul as a cooper taps a barrel.

If he feared any man – and this he was not prepared to admit, even to himself – he feared the little priest. Therefore he was careful with him, careful and courteous and humorously attentive as to a fellow exile on the outposts.

"Sit down, Father. Sit down. Get your breath back. Georgie will fix you a drink. My wife will be here presently. She has taken our friend Lansing to see the flowers."

"Madame is well?"

"Very well, thank you. The climate here is kinder to women than on the coast."

"She is still happy in the valley?"

Sonderfeld shot him a quick glance, but finding no malice in the bright eyes, he smiled and shrugged.

"If she is unhappy, she has not told me."

"Good, good. I have brought her an orchid. One of the big gold fellows. My boys found it in the gorge this afternoon."

He reached down into the canvas bag, took out the plant and laid it on the table. Its long, fleshy stalk

17

carried one full bloom and a row of bursting buds. Its roots were clotted in rich, black earth and bound in bark cloth. Sonderfeld smiled, approving the gentle gesture.

"Thank you. Gerda will be pleased. She has wanted one of those for a long time."

"'Ere's your drink, Padre," Wee Georgie shuffled over and laid the glass on the table. His hand trembled and a few drops splashed on the table-top. Sonderfeld frowned but said nothing. Père Louis looked up, grinning.

"You have the shakes again, Georgie."

Wee Georgie sniffed petulantly.

"Always 'appens when I'm on the wagon, Padre. Stands to reason don't it? A man's only flesh and blood."

"Try this, Georgie. It's easier on the liver than the native toddy."

The fat man's eyes lit up as the little priest produced a small bottle of altar wine. He reached out and, with a look of sidelong triumph at Sonderfeld, rammed it into the torn pocket of his trousers.

"That's charity, Padre. Real Christian charity. If there was anyone could get me singin' 'ymns at my age – which there ain't – but if there was, it'd be you."

Père Louis chuckled and waved him away. He raised his glass.

"*Santé, mon ami.*"

"*À la vôtre, mon père.*"

They drank comfortably, a pair of exiles twelve thousand miles from home. Sonderfeld offered a cigar. The little priest refused it, grinning as he produced a foul briar and a wad of trade tobacco.

"You would waste your cigar. I have smoked this stuff for so long, I cannot taste a good tobacco."

He lit up, puffing frantically to light the treacly plug. Then, when it was drawing comfortably, he said, "The tribes are still moving into the Lahgi Valley."

"I know." Sonderfeld's tone was indifferent, but he

was prickling with interest. "It's the usual thing, isn't it? They always come for the pig festival."

The Lahgi Valley was a great green crater over the lip of the northern barrier. Here was the principal village from which all the scattered colonies had spread over the surrounding mountains in search of new garden plots. Here they returned for the pig festival once every three years. Their coming was a mass migration spread over many weeks. When the festival was over, they would return to their own villages and their separate tribal lives. Sonderfeld's people had not yet begun to move; before they did, his preparations must be completed if his whole project were not to fall in ruins about his ears. Père Louis chewed irritably at his pipe and went on.

"As you say, it is the usual thing. But this time it is different. Something is stirring."

Now, thought Sonderfeld, now we come to the bones of it. He probed gently, cautiously, masking his anxiety with the tolerant smile of the philosopher.

"There is always something stirring in these people. They are restless as children. In the old times they could work it off with a war or a raid on their neighbour's taro patch. Now, they are controlled. The Administration disapproves of cathartic killings." He shrugged ironically. "Don't worry about it, Father. They will get rid of their fleas at the festival. They will sing and dance and get drunk, and come home quietly to cure their headaches."

"No." The little priest shook his head. "No, my friend, it is not so simple as that. You do not know these people as I do. They are not children. They are old – older than Greece and Rome, older than Babylon, old as the men who left their pictures in the sunken caves of the Pyrénées. Evil is rooted deep among them. Ancient evil, dark and frightening. It is stirring now. I know it, though I cannot put a name to it."

"But there must be signs, rumours –"

"There are signs – yes." He frowned. His weathered

19

face seemed suddenly shrunken and tired. "My Christians tell me the elders are saying that the Red Spirit himself will appear at the festival. He will come in human shape and will lead his people to prosperity and power beyond their dreams."

Sonderfeld chuckled tolerantly.

"The old, old wish-fulfilment. It appears in a thousand forms among the primitives and always at times of celebration or tribal crisis. It disappears as quickly – when the hangover starts. Look a little further you will find the rumour begins with some witch-doctor who wants to make a name for himself – and a profit, too, when all the people come together."

"I know the man already," said Père Louis flatly. "His name is Kumo. He lives in your village."

"Kumo, eh?" He must be interested now, but not too interested. "I have heard of him of course, as one hears of tribal identities. I have never paid any attention to him. A local charlatan, a little more intelligent than his fellows. How can such a man be important?"

"Kumo," said the priest, carefully. "Kumo was one of my mission boys. He was intelligent beyond the average. I hoped that he would become a catechist and even, one day, a priest – the first, possibly, from the Highlands here. Then there arose" – he hesitated, groping for words –" a problem of conscience. I cannot tell you what it was since it came to me under the seal of the confessional. I pointed out to Kumo what he must do. He refused. I denied him the Sacraments. He left me – left the Mission, too. He went up to the mountains to the teachers of the old, dark mysteries. He became a sorcerer." Again Père Louis paused, as if reluctant to put the thought into words. "I – I have reason to believe that he sold his soul to the Devil."

Sonderfeld exploded into laughter.

"No, no, no, Father! Not from you! You are too intelligent for that! Werewolves in Carinthia, with the village priest as ignorant as his flock? A scrubby curate in

20

Sicily with his weeping Madonna! But not from you. You are too wise, too old for this – this *Kinderspiel.* Look – we can be frank with each other. After all –"

"Mother of God !" Père Louis crackled into fiery anger. "How great a fool can a man be ! You sit there rocking on your chair laughing – at what? The monstrous evil of ten thousand years."

Sonderfeld was swift in apology. He had made a mistake. The luxury of laughter would come later. He could not afford it yet.

"Forgive me, my friend. I was tactless. I did not mean –"

Père Louis shook his head. His anger died as suddenly as it had quickened. His voice was sombre and sad.

"I know very well what you mean. Evil is an accident of the cosmos. The cosmos itself is an imperfect evolution of primal chaos. God is a name without substance. Satan is a medieval myth – Bah !" He took the pipe out of his mouth and laid it on the table. Hands and voice and eyes pieced out the low, passionate exposition. "Look, Kurt, try to understand. For your own sake, not for mine. I am too old to be troubled by laughter. But I am afraid for you. You cannot dismiss the mystery of creation with a shrug and a phrase. No man is big enough for that."

"You will forgive me if I doubt your explanation of it."

"Doubt it if you must; but do not dismiss it. Look !" There was a note almost of pleading in the old voice. "You know how I live here. You know how long I have lived here. I have no plantation as you have. I have no wife as you have. Yet I could have enjoyed them both, as you do now. Why did I choose to give them up? Because I believe in God and I believe in the Devil. I know that they exist, really, personally, actively. That is the whole meaning of a priest's life. To serve God and to fight the Devil – and to strengthen his flock to the same service and the same struggle."

"It is a notable belief, Father. It is also a harsh one.

21

It is my loss, perhaps, that I cannot accept it. I have never seen God. I have never seen the Devil. Until I do. . . ." He shrugged, eloquently.

"The footprints of God are on every acre of your valley. His handiwork is there on your table." He lifted the golden orchid bloom and held it up for Sonderfeld to examine.

Sonderfeld waved it aside.

"And the Devil, Father? Where do you see the Devil?"

Something akin to pity showed in the bright, wise eyes.

"If I were to tell you, my friend, that I have seen women dash the brains from their first-born and turn calmly to suckle a pig, if I were to tell you that there are magicians in the moutains – and this Kumo is one of them – who change themselves into cassowary birds and travel between the villages faster than man can run, if I were to tell that I have seen a girl suspended in the air, so that six men could not drag her down, that I have heard her screaming curses in the Latin of Saint Jerome while I, myself, pronounced the exorcism – and she a mountain girl who could not even speak pidgin – what would you say then?"

"Then," said Sonderfeld blandly, "then, Father, I should say that you have lived longer than I – and a good deal less comfortably. Now, if you'll excuse me, I will fetch my wife."

He heaved himself out of his chair. The little priest stayed him with a gesture.

"A moment, please."

"Yes?"

"You are concerned in this."

"I? How am I concerned?" His voice was harsh but steady.

"As I came up the path I met N'Daria. She was dressed for the sing-sing tonight."

"And how does that concern me? The girl belongs here. It is natural that she should want to join in the amusements of her own people. Even if I wished, I have no authority to prevent her."

"There is no question of prevention," said the old priest wearily. "It is simply that N'Daria is the chosen lover of Kumo. I thought you should know that."

"Thank you, Father." Sonderfeld's voice was cold. "Now that I know, I find it interests me not at all. Georgie! A drink for Père Louis. Forgive me, I shall not be a moment."

He turned on his heel and walked into the cool half-light of the house. Wee Georgie poured himself a double slug of whisky and tossed it off in one furtive gulp.

Père Louis sat slumped in his chair, staring out across the valley and the lengthening shadows of the mountains.

CHAPTER 2

GERDA SONDERFELD'S garden was a riotous miracle of colour and bursting life.

Two garden-boys, the summer rains, the tropic warmth, the mountain cool, and Gerda's own careful hands, had turned a quarter-acre of black volcanic soil into a private Eden.

Here in the high valleys there is no quartering of the seasons, no cyclic symbol of childhood and youth and maturity and age. Here there are only the big rains and the small, the sun in Cancer, the sun in Capricorn. Here you may plant what you will and when it pleases you. It will burst into life, bud, flower, as if in a forcing-house.

In Gerda Sonderfeld's garden there were salvias, red as live coals, gladioli with long spears and monstrous velvet blooms, beyond the avarice of temperate gardeners. There were dahlias and delphiniums, tall poppies and asters and white trumpet vines, giant coleus with mottled leaves, crotons and pied lilies, rock orchids and drooping ferns, and a passion vine trailing over a bamboo summer-house. There were casuarina-trees and clumps of bamboo, and shrubs with berries, red, purple, and shining orange. There were plants that might have graced an English garden, and wild grotesques that belonged only to the jungles and the rain-forests. The air was still and heady with perfume.

It was a masterwork, as full of contradictions as the woman who planted it.

She was in the summer-house now, with Max Lansing.

She smoothed down the bright cotton frock, moulding it back over her full breasts and downward to where it flared away from the roundness of her hips. Then she repaired her smudged lips and rearranged her dark hair in the small formal bun on the nape of her neck. Lansing watched her, impatient and puzzled.

A moment ago she had been in his arms, clinging to him, pressing his mouth down upon her own, exciting him almost to frenzy with the urgent straining of her tight strong body. Then, suddenly, she had thrust him away without regret or apology and begun this maddening little ritual of the toilet.

The passion had died in her, abruptly as a light dies when the current is switched off. The flush was gone from her skin, leaving it smooth as old, fine ivory. Her small hands were steady and patient in the intimacies of restoration. Her dark eyes were enigma. He could not tell whether they mocked or caressed him. Her parted lips were cool and dry.

Yet she was neither capricious nor a coquette. There was a bluntness in her desire, a blandness in her acceptance that had shocked him at first, then pricked him to greater need. It was the suddenness of the transformation that angered him and affronted his vanity. His own nerves were ragged and screaming with want. She was calm and comfortable as a kitten on a hearth-rug. He made as if to take her in his arms again. She moved a step beyond his reach still pinning up her hair.

"No, Max. Not now. Kurt will be here any minute. It would be embarrassing for all of us."

"Embarrassing!" It was as if the word gagged him. His flat mid-western voice was full of disgust and petulant anger. "Goddammit, Gerda! What do you think I am? I love you, don't you know that?"

"Keep your voice down, Max," she said calmly. "I can hear you. There is no need to shout at me."

"I'm not shouting. I'm trying to make you see —"

"But, darling, I see everything very plainly."

She patted the last hairs into place, then reached up and laid a cool hand on his cheek. The maternal gesture irritated him and he drew back from it abruptly.

"Okay! You see everything. You understand everything. Do you understand how much I love you? Do you understand what it's like to lie in my hut and listen to those goddamn' drums night after night, while you're up here with him? If I could just pack up and take you out of here...."

She smiled at him then — the tolerant, pitying smile of the adult for the stamping child.

"But you can't, can you, Max? You must stay here until your term is out — otherwise you lose the grant from the University. And even if you could, where would you take me?"

"Home — to the States."

She shook her head.

"To what? To a little apartment in a big city? To a little cottage near the campus? I would stifle there. Besides, for me, it would be hard to enter the United States. Be sensible, my dear. Let us enjoy the little we have. Look, tonight, if Kurt goes down the village, you can come to me —"

"For God's sake, Gerda!"

His anger went out like a snuffed candle. He stood before her, shoulders stooped, arms dangling, in an attitude of weary despair. Looking at him, she thought how sick and tired he was. His face was lined and yellow with suppressed malaria. His long, bony fingers were discoloured with tobacco. His clothes hung loosely over his big bones. His eyes were hollow and burning. Soon, she thought, he would be old and all his dreams would have cheated him. One day he would go home with his notes in a little canvas bag and his heart still hungry in his gangling body, and he would write his thesis and give his modest lectures and they would raise no ripple on the wide waters. For Max Lansing would always be the wrong man in the wrong place – too late, too early. His plans a little out of scale, his work out of rhythm, his life lonely and out of kilter.

Sudden pity took hold of her and she caught his hands and raised them gently to her lips. He bent over her and smelt the perfume of her hair.

"Listen to me, Max !" Her voice was gentle. He caught the faint gutturals that marked her for an alien. "I have said this to you before, I say it again. You are not meant for this sort of life. You are not one of those who can live alone. Give it up. Go home. Find yourself a nice American girl who will keep your house and give you children –"

"I can't go home." It was almost a cry. "This is my big chance. Don't you see that? This is one of the few places in the world where a research man can break new ground. If I can stick it out, I can make a name for myself, get myself a Chair at one of the big colleges –"

"All right, Max, all right." She had no heart to rob him of this last illusion. "But if you must stay, then at least accept what is here. Make yourself comfortable. Get yourself a village girl to look after you." She smiled up at him. "You would learn more from her in a week than you would in a year alone."

He thrust her away roughly.

"And come to you afterwards? Hold you in my arms? Make love to you?"

She shrugged and spread her hands in a small disarming gesture.

"Why not? It would not worry me. If you were content, I should be glad for you."

"And you say you love me!"

He turned away and began to fumble, defensively, for a cigarette.

"I have never said I loved you, Max," said Gerda quietly.

He whirled to face her.

"What then? In God's name, Gerda, what sort of a woman are you?"

She was still smiling. She would neither break nor bend nor give any hint of need to match his own.

"My husband," she said quietly, "calls me a whore. And yet I do not think I am. I have need of tenderness, as I have need of food, of the flowers in my garden. Kurt does not give it to me. I take it where I find it."

"From me or from the next man!"

"That's right, Max. From you or from the next man. Admit at least that I am honest about it."

"Sure, sure, you're honest about it!"

He let out a long, shuddering breath and ran his fingers through his cropped hair.

"Well ... thanks for telling me. I know where I stand now. I guess I'd better push off."

"My dear fellow," said Kurt Sonderfeld from the doorway, "you can't leave now. You are our guest. Your room is prepared. The others are expecting you. Shall we go in, Gerda?"

There were two new arrivals sitting in the canvas chairs drinking Wee Georgie's iced whisky – a blond youth in stained khaki, and a round, ruddy-faced fellow, immaculate in starched shirt and tropic shorts. They had come up from the Kiap house, a large thatched hut on the edge of the village, built and maintained by the tribe as a staging-camp for the officers of the Administration.

The blond youth was Lee Curtis, cadet patrol officer under the command of the District Commissioner at

Goroka His appointment constituted him policeman, judge, census-taker, and semi-military controller of three thousand square miles of territory and fifty thousand human beings. He had blue eyes and a baby mouth, and he sweated uneasily in the polyglot company of his elders. His frank adoration of Gerda was a constant amusement to Sonderfeld.

His companion was a Britisher, representative of an international coffee combine, investigating the resources of the Highlands under the auspices of the Agriculture Department of the Trustee Territory. He had the bland and easy manner of the seasoned traveller. He smiled continually, but his eyes were wary and shrewd behind his horn-rimmed spectacles. His unlikely name was Theodore Nelson. He was an expert in crop estimates and the diseases of the coffee plant, but his principal value to his employers was as a canny judge of the men who would one day come to them for finance, when the thrips destroyed a crop or the cost of clearing caught up with their bank balance.

They stood up, smiling, when Gerda came in, and shuffled for positions as Sonderfeld ushered her into the company with practised charm. Each of them wanted the chair beside her and Sonderfeld was bleakly amused when she ignored their invitations and settled herself beside Père Louis and eagerly began to admire the golden orchid. Still they could not take their eyes off her. The panic unease was stirring them as wind stirs a wheat-field, as the kundu drums stir the heavy silence of the uplands.

Strange, thought Sonderfeld sourly, that a woman could set fires in other men, and yet be colder than stone to the man who married her.

The reflection irritated him. He put it away and turned to the entertainment of his guests.

"You have seen my coffee, Mr. Nelson. What do you think of it?"

The Englishman was enthusiastic.

"Excellent! Excellent! I can safely say it is one of the best plantations I have seen on the Highlands. The soil is good and well manured. You have chosen the best shade-trees. I watched your boys spraying. You have trained them well."

Sonderfeld nodded, acknowledging the professional compliment.

"I made a close study of the problems before I opened the land here. The soil is rich. The climate is perfect. Given normal care, there is no reason why this country cannot produce the best coffee in the world."

"There is one thing that worries me," said Nelson carefully. "At least, it may worry the Company, should we ever come to do business together."

"What is that?"

"You have no road. You are fifty miles from Goroka. How are you going to get your crop out to the market?"

Lee Curtis cut in, stammering a little in his eagerness to join the discussion.

"Tha-that's what everybody in the Highlands would like to know. It-it's been a sort of a standing joke ever since Sonderfeld came up here. All the rest of the settlers took up land along the road. There's three hundred miles of it from Lae to Mount Hagen. Even the old hands in the Territory wouldn't come out as far as this."

Sonderfeld smiled tolerantly. This was an old question. It had long since ceased to be dangerous to him.

"There, in part at least, is the answer to your question, Mr. Nelson. This is the newest country in the world – the least exploited. Germany held it first, but before she could capitalize her holding, it was taken from her with the rest of her colonial empire. The League of Nations handed it over as a Mandate to the Commonwealth of Australia. Then the Japanese came and occupied the northern coast and some of the hinterland for the best part of the Pacific War. When Japan was defeated, Australia resumed the Administration under a new Mandate from United Nations."

29

Nelson looked puzzled.

"I don't see what that's got to do with the economics of coffee."

Sonderfeld smiled tolerantly.

"You would be surprised how much it has to do with coffee, my dear fellow. The Administration is a trustee, not an owner in perpetuity. As a trustee her prime duty is the welfare of the indigenous people. Under the terms of the United Nations Mandate, land must not be alienated permanently from the native population in favour of private individuals. Land which is not essential to the tribes may be acquired by the Government and leased by them for terms up to ninety-nine years. I was a late-comer. By the time I was ready to acquire a lease, the best land – that which borders the Highland road – was already pre-emptied. So, I had to move farther out. As you have seen yourself, I have not done badly."

"No," said Nelson dubiously. "But you still have the problem of getting your crop out. Load the freights too high and you price yourself out of the market."

Sonderfeld shook his head.

"I am not so short-sighted as that, believe me. By the time my crop is ready to flush, I shall have a road – my own road."

"You'll build it yourself?"

"My people will build it for me," said Sonderfeld calmly.

Père Louis looked up sharply. Max Lansing started, as if at a montrous revelation. Only Nelson and the young patrol officer seemed to find nothing strange in the simple assurance of their host.

Nelson looked inquiringly at Curtis. The youth nodded agreement.

"It could be done – provided the tribes co-operate, of course. At the moment they're very co-operative." He laughed loudly, like a self-conscious schoolboy. "Hope they stay that way. Makes my job easy."

Sonderfeld bowed in ironic acknowledgement.

"A compliment from the Administration! Thank you, my friend. Unfortunately, it would seem Père Louis does not agree with you."

"Oh? Why not?" Curtis rose truculently to the bait. The Missions were an old blur in the pelt of the Administration. The doctrine of the immoral soul raises more than one problem for colonial officials.

Père Louis chewed on his pipe. His eyes were veiled. His mouth was an enigma behind the square, Trotski beard.

Theodore Nelson studied him with mild disapproval. He had the Englishman's distaste for clerics who ventured beyond the cathedral close. There was a time and place for everything, and the Gospel of Saint John needed organ voluntaries and gothic gloom to make it half-palatable. Among the stone-age men it was Gallic indiscretion.

Père Louis looked up. His answer was mild and without emphasis.

"I happened to mention to our friend that the tribes are restless. The pig festival is approaching, as you know. The sorcerers are spreading rumours that the Red Spirit will appear in person at the time of the big sacrifice."

"So, that's it!" Lansing almost leapt from his chair. His voice cracked like a dry stick. The others looked at him in amazement. Only Sonderfeld seemed unmoved. He questioned Lansing with quizzical irony.

"Come, come, my friend. Don't tell me it surprises you. You live with these people, don't you? It is your profession to study the social patterns of primitive peoples. You must have heard these rumours as Père Louis has?"

"Sure, sure, I've heard 'em."

"Père Louis tells me they begin with a man named Kumo, a sorcerer in my own village."

"I disagree with Père Louis!"

Lansing was tight as a fiddle-string. His chin was

31

thrust out in nervous challenge. He was like a fighter moving in to his first opening. Sonderfeld was still smiling, but his eyes were wary.

"I am sure Père Louis would be glad to hear your views."

Lansing grinned.

"They might interest the Administration as well."

The patrol officer looked up. His boyish face took on an expression of comic gravity.

"We're always interested in the views of local residents. They help us considerably in making our own appreciation of the situation.

Lansing spread his long, bony hands and laid them finger-tip to finger-tip in a careful academic gesture. He was silent a moment, choosing his words. The others watched him silently. Gerda's eyes were troubled. Then he spoke, slowly, flatly, precisely.

"It is my considered opinion that the coming pig festival will be the occasion for an outbreak of the cargo cult in this area."

His words dropped into the silence like pebbles counted into still water. A ripple of interest stirred the small company. It was Theodore Nelson who spoke first.

"Cargo cult? That's new to me."

Lee Curtis was eager to explain.

"The cargo cult is –"

Lansing brushed aside the interruption and plunged into his own exposition.

"The cargo cult has many forms, but in essence it is very simple. It is the direct result of the impact of modern civilization on primitive man. The coming of the white man has revealed to the tribes a new heaven and a new earth, a way of life beyond their attainment. Time was when a man's wealth was measured by the number of his pigs or by his store of gold-lip shell. His manhood was rated by his skill in battle and the tally of his slain enemies. Now, tribal killings are a crime. The boys who come back from the coast after serving their indentures are discontented. They have seen bicycles and automobiles and refrigerators and moving pictures. They are no longer satisfied with pigs and trochus shell. The glory of the plumed head-dress and the sing-sing costume is a matter of secret contempt. Knowledge has come into Eden, and Adam is ashamed of his naked-ness."

He paused, gauging their interest, savouring the secret discomfort of Sonderfeld. Then he went on :

"That is the beginning of the cult – the new need, the new heaven beyond the stretch of dark fingers. Next comes the new prophet of the new promise. He uses the old symbols – the Pig God, the Red Spirit. He practises the old magic, the old rituals of sacrifice and propitiation. But the promise is new – 'Follow me and I will give you the riches of the white man, a share in the powers of the white man. The great droning birds will fly at my command. The cargoes they carry will be cargoes of wealth for you.' Ask any of the old hands. They will tell you of Black Christs and Black Kings. They will tell you how American Negro troops were hailed as libera-ting legions. Ask Patrol Officer Curtis, here, and he will tell you of wireless houses with vines for aerials and little armies carving wooden guns like those of the native police-boys."

He broke off, a little breathless from the fervent mono-logue. Then he made his final sober summation.

"That is how I read these rumours of the Red Spirit and his promised revelation at the pig festival. To this point, I believe, Père Louis will agree with me."

The little priest nodded, still chewing on his pipe.

"But," said Lansing, "this is where I disagree with him. The prophet is not Kumo. Kumo is the mouthpiece. The voice is the voice of another."

"What other?" Père Louis' question was deceptively mild.

Lansing turned to him and jabbed an emphatic finger at his shirt-front.

"You have lived in the Territory longer than any of us, Father. You know how often trouble among the tribes has been fomented by white men for their own ends – by gold-seekers and labour exploiters and crazy king-makers, who think that a mountain barrier can stop the march of civilization and enlightenment."

"I know it – yes," said Père Louis placidly. "I know also that their power has been brief and their end violent. Are you suggesting that the man behind Kumo is a white?"

"I'm stating it as a fact," said Lansing bluntly.

Darkness had come upon them unawares. The first stars were pricking out, low and bright, in the purple sky. As if to set a dramatic period to Lansing's speech, the black drums thudded into rhythm across the valley. Caught in the sudden mystery of the moment, no one spoke.

They dined by candlelight in the long room that look-shattered the illusion.

"From here to the Lahgi Valley and fifty miles north there are only five whites – Père Louis, Mr. Lansing, myself, Mrs. Sonderfeld –"

"And me !" said Kurt Sonderfeld. Then he laughed, a great deep bellow that rang out over the throbbing counterpoint of the kundus.

He was still laughing when he made up his mind to kill Max Lansing.

They dined by candlelight in the long room that looked out beyond the valley to mountains and the rich sky. The table was dressed with fine linen and silverware, and flowers from Gerda's garden. At each place was laid a single bloom of scarlet hibiscus. The wine glowed in long goblets of Bohemian crystal.

The servants were tall mountain boys in starched laplaps that made a small rustling as they padded about on silent, naked feet. The candles glowed on their brown breasts and the rippling muscles of their shoulders.

34

The tension that had built up between Sonderfeld and his guests relaxed under the suavity of good food and wine and conversation that ranged beyond the mountain barriers to the old countries over the sea. The drums were still throbbing in the village; but they were muted now, and distant, subdued to monotone like the beat of surf on a sheltered beach.

Here, in the shadowy room under the grass thatch, was Europe – Europe of the old, decaying beauties, of the checker-board frontiers, of the buried empires, Europe of the subtle centuries. Here woman was enthroned, soft under the candlelight, warm over the wine, smiling on her small court of churchman, trader, scholar, and functionary, served by her dark, dumb slaves from the outer march.

Sonderfeld watched them as they bent to her, laughed at her small jokes, preened themselves to her coquetries. Theodore Nelson forgot his caution and told her stories of his travels in Brazil and Africa and Ceylon. Père Louis poured out his drolleries of mission life; while Lee Curtis rummaged in his shallow grab-bag for trifles to divert her. Only Lansing refused his tribute. He sat, silent and resentful in the buzz of talk, while Sonderfeld watched him and sipped his wine and measured the harm that this unhappy man might do to him.

Gerda herself was a woman transformed. The brooding calm that normally enveloped her was shed like a cloak, revealing a nature of warmth and vitality. Her eyes sparkled, her gestures were vivid and expressive. As she became excited, she lapsed into little gaucheries of accent and idiom that added sauce and charm to her talk. The candlelight gave life to her ivory skin and made deep shadows in the curve of her throat and the hollow between her breasts. Small wonder, thought Sonderfeld, that other men desired her, when he himself could still be moved to fruitless want.

When the meal was over they tuned the radio to music from Moresby, and Gerda danced with Curtis and Nelson and Lansing, while Père Louis and Sonderfeld sat by the big window with coffee and brandies. They heard the tinkle of the music and the shuffle of the dancers and the occasional burst of laughter from Gerda; but under it all was the kundu beat, louder now and faster, as the drummers sweated over the black snake-skin.

Sonderfeld selected a cigar, slipped off the band, and pierced the butt with more than usual care. The drums were making him restless again. His nerves were frayed by the vapid chatter behind him. The memory of the scene on the stoop nagged him with its insistent warning of danger. He needed time and solitude to compose himself and complete his plans. Yet he was forced to play out this little comedy of leisure and good manners.

Cradled in a chair three sizes too big for him, Père Louis puffed contentedly at his pipe and studied his host through the smoke haze. For a long time now he had been worried over the big man. Outside he was hard and polished as teak wood, but the worms were chewing at the core of him, and Père Louis had a care even for those who were not of his faith. That Sonderfeld was distant from his wife was plain enough, though he gave no sign of being jealous of her. But an unsatisfactory marriage was not enough to explain the cold pride, the urgent, disciplined ambition of the man. Carefully as a chess-player, Père Louis made his opening gambit of inquiry.

"You know, Kurt, I am very grateful for these evenings in your house."

"I am glad to hear it, Father," said Sonderfeld placidly.

"After all these years, you would think the need should grow less. It does not."

"The need for what, Father?" He was glad of this desultory, calm exchange. It soothed him to patience, gave him time to set his thoughts in order.

Père Louis shrugged.

"Comfort. The comfort of civilized food and good wine and music. Companionship. The talk of one's own people. Even the sight of a beautiful woman, the sound of her voice and of her laughter."

Sonderfeld grinned.

"I thought, Father, you renounced these things when you took your vows."

The priest made a wry gesture.

"To renounce is one thing. To stifle the need is quite another. I think perhaps it never dies until the body itself is destroyed. You should be very grateful for what you have here – a beautiful wife, a comfortable house, a serene living."

"Grateful?" He rejected the word with angry contempt. "Grateful? To whom? To myself, for what I have attained with brains and patience and courage? To my wife, who makes herself a harlot in my own house? To these who eat my food and drink my liquor and lust after my woman? To the tribes who would steal the last shovel from my store if they were not afraid of me? To the country which would devour my coffee in a month if I were not here to keep it in check?"

If Père Louis was shocked by the outburst, he gave no sign. He shot a quick glance over his shoulder to see if the others had heard. They were still laughing and chattering and tapping their feet to the music. Gerda was pouring another round of drinks. He turned back to Sonderfeld. His canny eyes were hard. His mouth was grim.

"My friend," he said softly, "you are a very unhappy man."

"You are mistaken, Father. I am not unhappy. On the contrary, I am a very contented man. Why? Because I regard the follies of others as I regard the looseness of my wife – with contempt. They do not touch me. I have my own road to walk. I walk it alone and in peace."

"Alone, yes. But not in peace. And where does it lead, this road of yours?"

Sonderfeld grinned crookedly and shook his head.

"Oh, no! I am too wise a fox for that. You will not

bring me to your confessional, Father. Try my wife. She was a Catholic once. You may be able to lead her back to the fold. When she is too old for lust, she may develop a taste for piety. Who knows?"

"You are a fool, Kurt Sonderfeld," said the little priest softly. "I know this road of yours, because I have seen many men walk it. I have heard them cry out in despair when it was too late to turn back. I know where it leads."

"Where?"

"To death," said Père Louis simply. "To death – and damnation."

He stood up, brushed the ash from his shirt, and stuffed his pipe in his pocket.

"I must leave you now. It is a long walk to the Mission. I have an early Mass."

Sonderfeld bowed ironically.

"I am sorry you have to leave. Remember that you are welcome here at any time."

Père Louis shook his head. His lined face was tired and sad.

"No, Kurt. I shall not come again unless you need me and call for me. But I will give you a warning."

"A warning?" Sonderfeld's eyes were hard as pebbles. His mouth was a thin, stringent line.

"Look, Kurt," the old man made a last, weary plea, "you tell me you are an unbeliever. The tribes on the other hand are believers. They believe intensely, passionately, in the old faiths. No matter that they are false, debased, cruel, they are part of the fabric of life for these people. For that reason, if for no other, their belief is stronger than your disbelief. If you tamper with it, if, in pride and ignorance, you try to turn it to your own advantage, it will destroy you. Believe me, it will destroy you utterly."

"Nonsense, Father!" said Sonderfeld, and smiled as he said it. He stood up. Père Louis heaved himself out of the chair and stood looking up into the stony, mocking face of the big German. Anger blazed in his old eyes and his voice was charged with the biblical menace of the prophets.

"Stay away from the tribes, Kurt. Stay away from Kumo and the sorcerers. You are dealing with matters you do not understand. To call up devils is a simple thing. To exorcise them, one needs faith, hope, charity, and the abundant mercy of God. Good night, my friend!"

Brusquely, Sonderfeld led him through the brief rituals of farewell, and shepherded him out of the house. He stood a long time on the veranda listening to the drums and watching the small bat-like shadow flapping homeward under the casuarina-trees. He felt no regret. He had rid himself of one possible obstacle to his plans. The next was Max Lansing. But his death was already written on the palm of his hand. Sonderfeld was prepared to wait a little longer.

He looked down at the laboratory hut. There was no light yet. N'Daria was still in the village. He shrugged indifferently. The nights were long for mountain lovers and the throbbing drums had not yet reached their climax.

CHAPTER 3

Down in the village they were making kunande.

There were perhaps a hundred of them, bucks and girls, squatting two by two round the little fires in the long, low hut. Behind them, in the smoky shadows sat the drummers, crouching over the kundus, filling foetid air with the deep, insistent beat that changed from song to song, from verse to refrain, with never a pause and never a falter.

The couples around the fires leant face to face and breast to breast, and sang low, murmurous, haunting songs that lapsed from time to time into a wordless,

39

passionate melody. And, as they sang, they rolled their faces and their breasts together, lip to lip, nipple to nipple, cheek to brown and painted cheek.

The small flames shone on their oiled bodies and glistened on the green armour of the beetles in their head-dress. Their plumes bobbed in the drifting smoke, and their necklets of shell and beads made a small clattering like castanets as they turned and rolled to the rolling of the drums.

The air was full of the smell of sweat and oil and smoke and the exhalation of bodies rising slowly to the pitch of passion. This was kunande, the public love-play of the unmarried, the courting time, the knowing time, when a man might tell from the responses of his singing partner whether she desired or disdained him. For this was the time of the woman. The girl chose her partner for the kunande, left him when she chose, solicited him if she wished, or held herself cool and aloof in the formal cadence of the songs.

N'Daria was among them, but the man with her was not Kumo. Kumo would come in his own time and when he came she would leave her partner and go to him. For the present, she was content to sing and sway and warm herself with the contact of other flesh and let the drumbeats take slow possession of her blood.

A woman moved slowly down the line of singers. She was not adorned like the others. Her breasts were heavy with milk, her waist swollen with child-bearing. Now she would throw fresh twigs on the fire, now she would part one couple and rearrange the partners. Now she would pour water in the open mouth of a drummer, as he bent back his head without slackening his beat on the black kundu. This was the mistress of ceremonies, the duenna, ordering the courtship to the desires of her younger sisters, dreaming of her own days of kunande when she, too, wore the cane belt of the unmarried.

The drumbeats rose to a wild climax, then dropped suddenly to a low humming. The singing stopped. The singers opened their eyes and sat rigid, expectant. Distant at first, then closer and closer and closer, they heard the running of the cassowary bird. They heard the great clawed feet pounding the earth – chuff-chuff-chuff – down the mountain path, through the darkness of the rain-forest, on to the flat places of the taro gardens and into the village itself. Tomorrow they would go out and see the footprints in the black earth. But now they waited, tense and silent, as the beat came closer and closer, louder than the drums, then stopped abruptly outside the hut.

A moment later Kumo the Sorcerer stood in the doorway.

He did not enter, stooping as the others had done under the low lintel. He was there, erect and challenging as if he had walked through the wall. He wore a gold wig, fringed with green beetle-shards. His forehead was painted green and the upper part of his face was red with ochre. His nose ornament was enormous, his feathered casque was scarlet and blue and orange. His pubic skirt was of woven bark and his belt was covered with cowrie shells. His whole body shone with pig fat.

The boy who had been singing with N'Daria rose and moved back into the shadows. N'Daria sat waiting. Then Kumo gave a curt signal to the drummers, and they swung into a wild loud beat as he moved down the hut and sat facing N'Daria. No word was spoken between them. They sang and moved their faces together as the others did, but N'Daria's body was on fire and the drums beat in her blood, pounding against her belly and her breasts and her closed eyelids.

Then, after a long time, slowly the drumbeats died and the fires died with them. Quietly the couples dispersed, some to sleep, some to carry on the love-play in a girl's house, others to seek swift consummation in the shadows of the tangkret-trees.

Kumo and N'Daria left the hut with them and walked through the darkness to the house of N'Daria's sister.

Here there was food and drink and a small fire, and when they had eaten, two of the drummers came in with two more girls and they sat in pairs, backed against the bamboo walls to make the greater love-play, called in pidgin "carry-leg".

Kumo sat with his legs stretched out towards the centre of the hut. N'Daria sat beside him, her body half turned to him, her thighs thrown over his left leg, his right leg locked over hers. Then began a long, slow ritual of excitement, tentative at first, then more and more intimate and urgent. At first, they sang a little, snatches of the kunande songs; then they laughed, telling stories of other lovers and scandalous doings in the village and on the jungle paths. They made laughing flatteries of one another's bodies and their skill in the arts of love. Then, gradually, their voices dropped and their whispers became fiercer and more desirous.

"Does the white man touch you like this?"

"No – no –" She lied and half believed the lie in the warmth of the moment.

"Is the white man as great a man as I am?" His fingers pressed painfully into her flesh.

"He is not a man. Beside you he is a lizard."

"If he touches you, I will kill him."

"I would want you to kill him."

"I will make his blood boil and his bones turn to water. I will put ants in his brain and a snake in his belly."

"And I will watch and laugh, Kumo."

He caught her to him suddenly. His nails scored into her body, so that she gasped with the sudden pain.

"What does he teach you there in the little hut?"

She buried her face in his shoulder to hide the small smile of triumph. Kumo was a great sorcerer, the greatest in the valleys. Kumo could change himself into a cassowary bird and travel fast as the wind. But even Kumo did not know the secrets she learnt in Sonderfeld's laboratory.

42

"Tell me. What does he teach you?"

She giggled and clung to him.

"What will you give me if I tell you?"

"I will give you the charm that makes children and the charm that destroys them. I will make you desired of all men. I will give you the power to strike any woman barren and make any man a giant to embrace you."

"I want none of these things."

His mouth was pressed to her ear, he whispered urgently so that the others could not hear.

"What do you want? Tell me and I will give it to you. Am I not the greatest sorcerer in the valleys? Does not the Red Spirit speak to me in the thunder and in the wind? Ask me and I will give. What do you want for the secrets of the white man's room?"

"Only that you should take me – now!"

His body shuddered with the flattery and the triumph of it.

"And you will tell me, when?"

"Tomorrow or the day after, when I can come without being seen. But not now – not now!"

Kumo laughed. His plumes tossed. His teeth shone. He swept the girl to her feet and half ran, half carried her out of the hut.

The consummation was a wild, brief frenzy that left her, bruised and crumpled, alone in the tall and trodden kunai grass.

The drums were silent, and the last fires were dying as N'Daria stumbled up the path to light the lamp in Sonderfeld's laboratory. Her body was aching and her head was swimming with fatigue and drunkenness, but between her belly and her belt was a piece of cotton-wool which carried the life of Kumo the Sorcerer.

Wee Georgie was waiting for his wives to come home. In the small, squalid hut on the edge of the track, he sat shivering under a ragged greatcoat, lamenting his misfortunes like Job on his dunghill.

First was the irregularity of his marriage, unblessed by the Church, the Administration or the tribes. The plump, brown sisters were happy enough to share his rations and warm his rumpled blankets, but they counted themselves still among the unmarried and went to the kunande and solaced themselves regularly with the village bachelors. Wee Georgie was a tolerant fellow, frankly admitting his own impotence, but the mountain nights were cold and his blood was so thinned with alcohol that he could not sleep without the companionable warmth of an oily body, fore and aft.

More than this, his kidneys were suffering from half a century of systematic abuse and he was forced to make repeated trips to the base of the big casuarina-tree while the cold seeped into the fatty marrow of him.

But worse than all, theme of the longest lamentation, was the liquor shortage. Père Louis' altar wine was thin comfort and soon gone – and Sonderfeld's ill-humour had robbed him of his week-end ration of hard spirit. There was only a quarter of a bottle of whisky between himself and the terrors of the night, and this he was saving until the girls came home, so that he could sit and listen to their spicy gossip of village love, and piece out the scraps of scandal that might one day earn him an extra bottle from Sonderfeld. It was the only pleasure left to him in the days of his decline, and he clung to it jealously, cursing the shameless lusts that kept his women late from his pillow.

A sharp pain in the region of his bladder brought him unsteadily to his feet, and he lurched out into the moonlight to relieve himself. He saw N'Daria stumbling wearily up the track and when he looked up towards the big bungalow he saw the big figure of Sonderfeld leaning on the veranda rail, and behind him, silhouetted against the window, the gesticulating shadows of three men in the lighted living-room. The girl must have gone to bed, leaving the men to drink late. He grinned lecherously and wondered how long she'd stay there.

44

Lansing would sleep at the house as he always did, and when the others had gone, Sonderfeld would come down to the laboratory and the lamp would burn long after midnight. Did he work there – or play? Wee Georgie had his own ideas, but he was wise enough to keep them to himself. This was the softest berth he'd had in many years, he wanted to keep it. Another mistake like to-night's could mean disaster.

He shivered and swore and reeled back into the hut. Then, far down the track he heard the pad of feet and the high giggling of the girls. He wondered whether he should beat them, but decided against it. He uncorked the bottle and took a long gurgling pull that ended in a belch of relief. Then he stretched himself out on the dirty blanket roll and waited for them to come in. With whisky in his belly and girls in his bed, Wee Georgie was the Caliph of the high valleys. He speculated amiably on the scandalous tales that Scheherazade and her sister would bring – he had a shrewd suspicion that N'Daria and Kumo would have their parts in it.

Sonderfeld saw the light go on in the laboratory and smiled to himself in the darkness. He was desperately eager to know the result of N'Daria's seduction of the sorcerer, but he was too careful a man to betray himself by even the smallest indiscretion. Gerda was safely in bed, but his guests were still drinking. He would go in to them, join the last hazy rounds, and tell them a dirty story or two to send them on their way to bed.

Lansing, he would conduct with ironic courtesy to the guest-room. With Curtis and Theodore Nelson he would walk a little way down the path that led to the Kiap house; he would tell them one last story; he would stand and watch them weaving homewards under the dark, drooping trees. Then, he would go to N'Daria.

He straightened up, tossed the butt of his cigar over the railing, and walked into the bright light of the living-room.

Theodore Nelson, flushed and voluble, had reached the tag of his story:

"She said to me, 'What sort of a woman do you think I am?' I said, 'My dear lady, I thought we'd already established that.' After which, of course, it was plain sailing from Aden to Bombay."

Lee Curtis gave his braying, boyish laugh. Max Lansing, grey-faced and weary, stared into his glass. They looked up as Sonderfeld came in, smiling and hearty.

"Forgive me, my friends. I was having myself a little fresh air between drinks. Now the clergy are gone and the lady is retired, let's have ourselves a private nightcap, eh?"

"If you don't mind," said Lansing flatly, "I'll take myself to bed. I'm very tired. I'm not good company."

"My dear fellow!" Sonderfeld was instantly solicitous. "Of course we don't mind. Are you sure you are not unwell? You're not getting the fever are you? Have you been taking the tablets?"

"No, no ... it's not the fever. I'm just tired, that's all. If you'll excuse me – good night, Sonderfeld. Good night, gentlemen!"

Before they had time to speak their own farewells, he had left the room, a tall, stooping figure bowed under the burden of his own ineptitude.

"That's an odd fellow," said Theodore Nelson, as Sonderfeld poured him a generous slug.

"They're all odd, these anthropology boys," Lee Curtis chimed in, with his shining new knowledge. "Lots of 'em scattered round the Highlands. Queer as coots. They –"

"You mustn't be too hard on the poor fellow." Sonderfeld's tone was a careful blend of tolerance, amusement, and genuine affection. "He's a clever and devoted scholar. A little prickly in company, of course, but that comes of living alone. Add to which he is a very sick man. He has had one bout of scrub typhus. If I had not been here, I think it would have killed him. Gerda and

46

I are very fond of him. That is why we like to have him here as often as we can."

Theodore Nelson clucked sympathetically and plunged his snub nose into his drink. His own reading of the Lansing story made a very different text. But when a man made his living drinking other men's whisky and eating at other men's tables it paid him to keep his thoughts to himself.

Lee Curtis was a less practised diplomat. Lansing's views on the cargo cult had been nagging at him all the evening. If they were correct, they spelt trouble for himself. The District Commissioner was a hard man and a subtle one. He had neither patience nor mercy for weak administrators and slipshod investigations. Curtis stifled a hiccup and put the question to Kurt Sonderfeld.

"He's a clever scholar, you say. But you laughed at his ideas on the cargo cult. Why?"

"My dear fellow," said Sonderfeld smoothly, "there is no contradiction, believe me. Lansing is a scholar, a man of books and theories. He lacks the practical experience of, say, a man like yourself."

Nelson grinned into his drink. You clever bastard, he thought. You clever, clever bastard. There's weather blowing up and you know it. Lansing knows it, too. But you're not making any forecasts. You're leaving it all to this boy, who hasn't finished cutting his milk-teeth. If there's storm damage, you'll be high and dry with a handsome profit.

Lee Curtis hiccuped again. The compliment was sweeter to him than the whisky and just as heady. He jabbed an unsteady finger at Sonderfeld's shirt-front. His voice was thick and furry.

"That's what I always say. It's the men that do the job that really know. You do it – in a small way – on your plantation. I do it – in a big way – in my territory.

47

The rest of 'em – the missionaries and the anthrop—anthrop—" He giggled, happily. "Christ, I'm drunk! Better take me home, Nelson, before I fall flat on my face."

Deftly, Sonderfeld manoeuvred him through the last drink, smiling like a genial conspirator at the moon-faced Britisher who had survived a thousand evenings like this one. Nelson was no danger to him. Nelson was a bird of passage, hovering high above the storm waters. Nonetheless, it would pay to keep him friendly. With Curtis swaying between them, they walked out of the house.

When the cold air hit him, the boy gagged suddenly and vomited on the path. In the darkness, Sonderfeld grimaced with disgust, but he handled the situation with the ease and competence of long experience. He locked one arm round the boy's waist, supported his head with his free hand and held him until the spasm had passed. Then he cleaned him with his own handkerchief and handed him over to Nelson with a good-humoured grin.

Nelson watched the performance with bibulous approval. The fellow was a gentleman at least. In his peripatetic career he had met a few originals and many imperfect copies, but Sonderfeld had earned the seal of the connoisseur. If it came to a show-down between the big man and the Administration, Nelson would back private enterprise every time.

Which was exactly what Sonderfeld expected him to do.

He stood a long time, watching, as their shadows swayed down the narrow path. Then he turned and walked swiftly back to the laboratory.

N'Daria was waiting for him.

She had stripped off the ceremonial costume, wrapped herself in an old housecoat that had belonged to Gerda. She was drooping with sleep and her body gave off the smell of fatigue and staling oil. There was no desire in

48

her smile, only a furtive triumph. She held out to Sonderfeld the evening's prize, carefully laid in a small tube
of bamboo.

He took it from her without a word, slid off the top of
the tube and gingerly extracted the wad with a pair of
tweezers.

Strange, he thought strange. Between those two steel
fingers he held the key to power and dominion. That
small foul relic of an animal act was a talisman whose
touch would call up armies, rear a throne in the mountains, set on the forehead of its possessor the crown of
a new empire. It was a giddy thought.

Yet it was true. The tribes were ruled in secret by
the sorcerers. Chief of the sorcerers was Kumo. The
man who held the blood and seed and spittle of Kumo
was greater than he because at any moment, by a
simple wilful act, he could compass the death of Kumo.
Such was the power of ancient superstition that once
Kumo knew his vital juices were held by another man,
he would be in perpetual bondage. Burn the tube in the
fire and Kumo's body would burn to agonizing death.
Crush the tube with an axe, Kumo would feel the stone
grind into his own skull and would die of the impact.
Warm it a little, beat on it with a stick, Kumo's body
would burn with fever or his ears would ring with
maddening noises.

It was the old, dark, fearful magic of primitive man
turned against him by a twentieth-century despot.

For a long time Sonderfeld stood there, lost in the
secret joy of his own triumph. The girl watched him,
smiling uneasily. Then, abruptly, he replaced the tampon, closed the tube with a snap, and thrust it into his
pocket. He turned to her and grinned.

"You have done well, N'Daria."

Her eyes lit up. She moved forward to touch him.
He drew back in disgust. It was as if he had struck her.

"But . . . But . . . you said. . . ."

"You stink !" said Sonderfeld softly. "You stink like a

village pig. Before you begin work in the morning, wash yourself clean."

With that he left her. She heard the door slam and the key turn in the lock. She flung herself on the low, cane bed and sobbed.

CHAPTER 4

GERDA was asleep when he came in.

She lay on her side, her face pillowed on one hand, the other lying slack across the curve of her hip. Her hair was a dark cascade against the white sheets. Her skin was like warm marble, her lips were smiling softly, like the lips of an innocent child. He turned up the lamp and stood looking down at her. She stirred faintly, then settled again, still smiling. It was as if she mocked him, even from the frontiers of sleep.

She had been with Lansing. He knew that. She had been as warm to him as she was cold to her legal partner. She had been tender and passionate and wanton – to a straw man, limp with his own self-pity. She had put horns on her husband in his own house and there was nothing he could do about it – yet. He could strike her and she would laugh in his face. He could kill her – as soon he would kill Lansing – but her death would bring him loss instead of profit. So he must wear the horns and endure the dreaming mockery night after night, until his triumph was perfected and she was delivered once more into his hands, as she had been that winter's day, twelve years ago ... when Sturmbannführer Gottfried Reinach stood in the compound at Rehmsdorf and slapped his cane against his polished jackboots and looked ed over the new batch of women from Poland.

There were more than fifty of them, old and young and in-between. They were dirty and in rags. Their faces were pinched with hunger, their eyes glazed with

50

fear. Their feet were bound with rags and old news-papers, and their skin was blotched with cold. They stood ankle-deep in the slushy snow, humble under the professional scrutiny of Gottfried Reinach.

He was an important fellow, the Sturmbannführer, ambitious too, and careful of his career. He held medical degrees from two universities. His brief civilian practice had given him the name of a brilliant pathologist. His repugnance to Army service and his desire for rapid advancement had turned his thoughts to politics. He had joined the Party. He had made good connections – right to the door of Himmler himself – and now he was established comfortably, almost spectacularly, as Chief Research Officer, with the rank of Sturmbannführer in Rehmsdorf concentration camp. Here, he directed the researches of a group of junior men on typhus vaccines, using as his subjects the decaying wrecks who were the camp inmates. He had other duties, too, the choice of subjects for the gas-chambers and for the Sonderbau, the sterilization of young woman of inferior race, lest child-bearing interfere with their duties or increase the per-centage of helots among the master-men.

He had little taste for the work or for his associates, but he was a calculating fellow and, having chosen his road, he walked it resolutely – and circumspectly. His files were carefully kept. His success was minuted to the highest authorities. His failures were stifled as soon as they were born.

So, on this winter's morning, he walked down the line of women like a buyer in a cattle-yard, pointing with his little stick, sorting them into categories – this for the work-commandos, that for the brothel, this other for the Officers' Mess, these for the scrap-heap. . . .

Until he came to the end of the line and saw Gerda Rudenko.

She was tattered and travel-stained like the others and the same fear was in her eyes, but her beauty was like a banner and her youth was still unravaged. She was a student, according to his lists. Her crime was consorting with suspected persons. She was nineteen years' old.

To Sonderfeld she was a percentage profit. He had her sterilized like the others. He had her examined with more than usual care for venereal and other diseases. Then he took her into his service – clerk by day, bed and body servant by night. She was diligent because she was afraid of him and of his power to consign her to the crematorium. Because he was kind to her sometimes and not too often cruel, she was grateful, tender when he permitted it, passionate when, more and more rarely, he touched the deep spring of desire in her young body. There were even moments when fear and need brought her almost to belief in him; but as the years of her servitude spun out and she came to know him more intimately, belief became impossible. She served him still, but only with fear and with a deep and hidden hate.

Then came the last wild madness of defeat, the frenzy of murder, when the bodies piled up in the compounds and the gas-chambers were choked, and the furnaces could not keep pace with the fuel that was fed to them. For the first time in his life, Gottfried Reinach was afraid – afraid of the haggard beasts in their wire pen, afraid of the vengeance that rolled in with the tanks and the gun-limbers and the troop carriers.

So he struck his bargain with Gerda Rudenko.

He would take her out of the camp, save her from the final holocaust. He would marry her – not as Gottfried Reinach, but as Kurt Sonderfeld, Doctor of Medicine, bachelor, dead long since and burnt in the fire; but Sonderfeld's records lay, complete and carefully preserved in the steel filing cabinet.

When the final collapse came they would merge themselves in the tide of stateless wanderers and claim protection from the liberating armies. And, lest she be tempted to accept now and betray him later, he pointed out that she, too, was compromised by her long association with Gottfried Reinach. She had enjoyed the protection of the defeated; she might well share their punishment.

She was trapped, and she knew it. She made the bargain. Three days before Rehmsdorf was taken, they left the camp. Reinach was now Sonderfeld. The dead man's number was tatooed on his forearm, the list of his works and days was etched in his memory. He wore the filthy rags of a camp inmate, starved himself for a week, and had Gerda shave his skull to complete the change of identity.

The plan worked. Slowly they sifted through the inadequate machinery of relief organizations and re-establishment camps. They answered questions and filled in papers and lived in daily fear of recognition, until one day their names were posted on the camp notice-board as migrants acceptable to the Commonwealth of Australia.

A new life was opening to Kurt Sonderfeld and his wife, Gerda. A new horizon challenged his cold ambition. This time he would follow no banners, he would walk alone.

They were a week out from Genoa when Gerda had her first affair with a fellow migrant. When he taxed her with it, she smiled. When he threatened her, she laughed in his face. When he struck her, she told him, gently and without anger:

"If you ever do that to me again, Kurt, I will tell everything I know. No matter what happens to me, I will tell. Remember that. We are bound together. We cannot escape each other. But from this moment I do not wish to sleep with you, to kiss you, even to touch you ever again."

At first he thought of divorcing her as soon as he could. Then he realized he would never sleep in peace so long as she was free and able to tell his secret. He toyed with the idea of killing her, but before he could frame a plan, she had forestalled him. They had not been two months in Australia when she told him that she had lodged papers with a bank – papers that would incriminate him if she should die before him.

No, it was he who was trapped, bound to a body he had maimed, denied its pleasures, shamed by its defiant wantonness.

As for Gerda herself, she was a woman without illusions. Cheated of love, cheated of children, she had made a bargain that guaranteed her security and comfort – and the bitter sweets of a protracted revenge. On this rickety foundation she and Kurt had built for themselves a kind of permanence, even a kind of peace. They were polite to each other. They co-operated on projects of mutual benefit. If they made love in other beds, they did so with reasonable discretion. In the new land bustling and bursting with vitality, they were accepted even if they were not loved.

One of the conditions of their entry into Australia was that they should serve, each of them, for two years in any employment to which they were directed. Sonderfeld worked as a tally clerk on a dam construction project, Gerda as a waitress in the men's canteen. Strangely, the big man was not irked by the humble work. He was learning the language, adapting himself to a new, rugged environment. Every scrap of information was scanned and filed away for future reference. He had made one mistake in his life; he was not going to risk another. Sometime, somewhere, in this young, thrusting country, a door would be opened to him and he must be ready to enter into his new estate.

Then one day he read a notice in a Government Gazette. Migrant Doctors who could produce evidence of medical qualifications in Europe would be permitted to practise in the Mandated Territory of New Guinea without renewing their courses.

This was his chance. He grasped it with both hands.

Within a month he and Gerda were in Lae. Within three years he had built a practice, a bank balance, and a reputation. He was offered a permanent appointment under the Administration. He refused, smiling. Kurt Sonderfeld had served long enough. Now he was ready to rule.

The rich Highland valleys were being opened up. Land was being leased to settlers of energy and good character. His application was approved – the more quickly because he was ready to push out over the mountains, where even the old hands were not prepared to risk their money.

So he had come to the valley, trekking over the mountains with Gerda and the cargo-boys. He had made friends with the tribes. He had earned the goodwill of the District Commissioner by his gratuitous care of their health. Within a year his ground was cleared, his house was built, his coffee was planted under the shade-trees – and his dream of wealth and empire was near to fulfilment.

The first step was the domination of the tribes through Kumo and the lesser sorcerers. The next was the exaction of tribute: labour, pigs, gold washed from the Highland streams, lumber from the rich stands in the tribal territories, a tithe of every man's garden patch, basket- and cane-ware, cinchona bark and galip nuts, to sell as the Missions did on the coast. Territory law compelled him to feed and clothe and pay his boy-labour, but these payments would be returned to him less a nominal deduction by the sorcerers for their sumptuary service. It was a grandiose project, but simple and feasible in practice. So long as he could keep peace among the tribes. Before the Administration caught up with him – if they ever did – he would be ready to quit. And this would be the final stage, the return of the freebooter, rich and acceptable, to the luxury of life in Europe.

Yet wealth alone was too low a peak for his leaping

pride. He must stretch out farther to the pinnacles of power. Power was an obsession with him – a brooding, secret lust that blinded him to the lessons of his personal and national history, and showed him only the sweet illusions of attainment.

In the isolation of the high valleys where authority was represented by puling boys like Lee Curtis, the prospect of imperial rule seemed dangerously possible.

There was no garrison strength in the Territory, only the small, scattered force of native police. Airfields were few and fit only for small aircraft. Communications were sketchy and unreliable.

There were thousands of square miles of unexplored country peopled by tribes who had never seen a white skin. For a bold man, a shrewd man, leagued with the sorcerers, there seemed no limit to the extension and exercise of god-like authority.

All this, and more, would flow, like wealth from Fortunatus' purse, out of the small, bamboo tube whose glossy surface shone dully in the lamplight.

Gerda stirred and murmured uneasily. He thrust the tube back into his pocket and began preparing himself for bed. Tonight he would rest well. Tomorrow was the beginning of a new chapter in the saga of Kurt Sonderfeld.

Five minutes later he, too, was asleep, smiling, like Gerda, in his golden dream.

It was two in the morning before Père Louis reached his Mission Station, a small, poor village sprawling along a narrow defile between Sonderfeld's property and the Lahgi Valley. To reach it, he had walked six miles along the flanks and the ridges of the mountains, through stretches of rain-forest and occasional patches of kunai grass taller than himself. As he walked, he prayed, fingering the worn beads of his rosary; and as he prayed, he pondered . . . on what he had heard in

Sonderfeld's house, on what he knew of the trouble simmering among the tribes.

Much of it was secret to himself. It came to him in whispers when his converts shuffled into the tiny chapel to make their confessions. This one had been threatened by the sorcerers and needed reassurance. Another had bought herbs to procure an abortion and begged absolution.

A boy had taken his girl into the bushes after the kunade and the carry-leg. His catechist demanded to know whether to take part in the pig festival was an act of idolatry or a harmless enjoyment of a village feast. But all the whispers were fragments of one story; the story of a wavering minority, clinging desperately to a new faith, afraid of the mockery of the old believers, more afraid of the dark powers of which they had daily, terrifying experience.

Père Louis himself was afraid. Not of the legends, not of the childish superstitions and the primitive spells, but of the ancient evil working in them and through them. He believed in the human soul. He believed in sin. He believed in God. He believed in the Devil who walked the valleys, not roaring like a lion of Saint Paul, but muttering and chanting, threatening and bribing, through the sorcerers.

Some of them were charlatans, as Sonderfeld had said. These he could ignore or discredit. But there were others, the powerful few like Kumo, intelligent, proud, dedicated to evil and the Prince of Evil. If, as he now believed, Sonderfeld had joined forces with them, the stirring in the valleys might grow to a whirlwind.

The big man puzzled him. He was not, like others, a wencher, chasing the village girls, a tippler, a ragged adventurer chasing gold or oil like folly-fires through the valleys. Sonderfeld was intelligent, cultivated, controlled. If he were to take a risk, it would be a calculated risk, and the reward would be calculated with greater care. The man was devoured by a cold pride and a ruthless ambition – but for what? Money, perhaps. But money was too low a goal for such a man. Power?

Père Louis shivered though he was hot and sweating from the walk. Power was the greed of Lucifer. The lust for power was the sin against nature and the Holy Ghost, the sin beyond mercy.

In the tiny, rustling chapel, lit by a guttering taper that floated in a bowl of oil, the priest lay prostrate in supplication before his God. The god of the tribes was a Great Pig and beyond the Great Pig was the Red Spirit. The God of Père Louis was the Crucified who lay on the crude altar in the form of white wafer of bread. The old man's lips framed the familiar cadence of the Office of Compline. . . .

"*Scuto circumdabit te veritas eius.* . . . His truth shall compass thee with a shield. Thou shalt not be afraid of the terror of the night."

"*A sagitta volante in die, a negotio perambulante in tenebris.* . . . From the arrow that flieth in the day, from the plague that walketh in darkness, and from the noonday devil. . . ."

In the high secret valleys the sorcerers cast their spells; Kurt Sonderfeld slept in his white bed and dreamed of dominion and power; but Père Louis prayed in his bamboo church until the stars waned and the sun crept up on the ridges and his catechist found him lying face down, exhausted, on the altar step.

CHAPTER 5

WEE GEORGIE was mustering the plantation boys. It was seven-thirty in the morning and they came loitering up from the village, torpid, red-eyed, scowling, to squat in little groups outside Wee Georgie's hut.

Stripped of their finery, their skins dull and dusty,

their teeth stained and their mouths drooling with betel juice, they were an unpromising crew.

Wee Georgie surveyed them with regal contempt and spat in the dust before them. He was leaning against the big casuarina-tree, an obscene and rumpled figure, with bleary eyes and the sour taste of hangover on his tongue. His shirt flapped raggedly outside his breeches, his belt hung precariously below his navel. His hair was a towy mess and his bare feet scuffed irritably in the dirt of the path. One trembling hand held a cigarette, the other scratched constantly under a sweaty armpit.

His two girls peered out of the doorway behind him and giggled softly. Their lord was in a fouler mood than usual. The performance would be worth watching.

The last stragglers arrived and stood shuffling uneasily under Georgie's baleful eye. He took a last long drag at his cigarette, coughed till he was purple in the face, and spat again.

Then he started.

"On your feet you black bastards! Get into line. Jump to it!"

Slowly they heaved themselves up from their haunches and moved into file in front of him. His ugly face twisted into a grin; he took a deep breath and began to curse them, softly and fluently. He cursed them in pidgin and place-talk and bawdy Billingsgate. He cursed them for the colour of their skins and the lechery of their women; he cursed them by the names of birds and beasts and crawling things; he cursed them as eaters of the dead and crammers of offal. They were a stink in his nostrils, an offence to his sight, an obscene pollution of the mountain air. They coupled with pigs and brought forth monsters. Their fingers were a black blight on the coffee and when they died, even the ants would reject their foul carcasses.

By the time he had finished, they were grinning all over their dark faces. Their ill-temper was dissipated and they nodded to one another, approving this intoxicating eloquence. But this was only the beginning, the overture to the comedy.

Wee Georgie hawked again. A great gob of spittle landed at the feet of a tall buck and threw up a puff of dust as high as his ankles. The boys guffawed happily. The girls squealed with shrill delight. Georgie eased himself away from the tree-bole and lurched over to his target. Slowly, he surveyed him from his frizzy crown to his scrabbling toes, and began his gallery speech.

"This is Yaria. This is Yaria who talks like a taro root and performs like a bud of bamboo."

The boys hooted with laughter. Yaria was a well-known boaster, whose girls were never satisfied. The white man was a clever fellow who knew all the gossip of the village. Wee Georgie grinned happily. His play was running well.

"This Yaria was at the kunade last night. He changed partners three times – and still couldn't find a girl to sleep with him."

There was laughter and jeering while Yaria hung his head and scuffed his feet in embarrassment.

"Yaria wants to get married and have a son. But he can't find the bride-price – and even if he did, he'd need another man to help him –"

And so on, through the cheerful ritual of obscenity and insult until the sullen workers were bubbling with good humour and filled with gossip enough to last them through the working day. When he had finished with Yaria, Georgie moved to the next man in the line, and the next, spitting at their feet, parading them like hacks in the knacker's yard, spreading his ridicule so that no man escaped and none could feel resentment or loss of face.

It was a canny performance that guaranteed him the goodwill of his labour force and gave him leisure to sit in the shade with his straw hat tipped over his eyes, while the boys moved up and down the lines of trees, cultivating, spraying, clearing the irrigation ditches, and chewing the spicy cud of the morning's entertainment.

He was nearly at the end of the line when he saw Kumo. The big fellow was standing a little apart from the others, arms folded on his chest, his face a blank mask, his eyes full of cold hatred.

Wee Georgie shivered and his tirade limped to a close.

Hurriedly, he set them their tasks – these to the sprays, these others to the new clearing, half a dozen to the drainage ditches from the upper pond, two to rake the paths and clip the lawns, the rest to weed and mulch the coffee rows.

Grinning and chattering, they dispersed to pick up their tools and start work. Kumo stood aloof and impassive as if challenging the fat man to assert his authority. Wee Georgie was too shrewd to engage the sorcerer.

"You wait there, big boy. The boss wants to see you," he snarled.

Then he spat contemptuously and lurched back to the hut where the girls were making his breakfast.

Kumo squatted at the foot of the casuarina-tree and waited for Sonderfeld to come to him.

The big man walked slowly down the path, flicking at his calves with a thin switch of cane. It was a gesture that, in another time and another country, might have betrayed him. It recalled the shining jackboots and the trim black uniform of a discredited elite. Here in the bright mountain morning it was meaningless as brushing away flies.

As always, his arrival was carefully timed to coincide with the end of Georgie's oration and the dispersal of the boys. They would see him coming the full length of the path, and they would stumble over one another in their eagerness to get to work and avoid the disapproval of his cold stare. Their fear flattered him and fed the fires that consumed him.

This morning his entrance was staged with even

greater care. When he saw Kumo on his hunkers in the dust, he stopped and spent long minutes examining the big coleus plants that bordered the path. He took a cigar from his pocket and lit it with care and deliberation, before he resumed his walk.

As he walked, he rehearsed the scene he was about to play. He would not use pidgin, which was the language of subjection, nor English which was the language of equality. He would speak to Kumo in his own tribal tongue, and this would say more clearly than words : "I know you. You cannot deceive me with a double tongue or with the blankness of ignorance. I share your secrets and yet I am greater than you."

He would speak privately, in the shelter of the tangket-trees, so that the sorcerer would not be humbled and lose face with his fellows. His influence must be preserved, while his will was bent and his spirit humbled to the service of Sonderfeld. He would rebel, of course. He would rear against the yoke, because he was a proud man. Because he was an intelligent one, he would try to bargain, shrewdly, deviously, with the threat of betrayal to the patrol officer and the Administration. But Sonderfeld would reject the bargain and break the rebellion.

He grinned crookedly and fingered the bamboo tube in his pocket. He wondered what Kumo would do when he saw it for the first time.

The sorcerer did not stir when Sonderfeld came up to him. He remained squatting against the tree, eyes downcast, his jaws champing on the cud of betel nut. Sonderfeld stood a moment, watching him, then he flicked the cane switch sharply across his cheek. Kumo's head came up with a jerk. His eyes blazed.

"Get up," said Sonderfeld softly. "Come with me. I want to talk to you."

Then he turned away and walked into the shelter of the trees out of sight of the hut and of the house. Slowly, Kumo got to his feet and followed him.

In the dappled shadow under the purple leaves, they

faced each other, black man, white man, each master in his own domain.

Sonderfeld smiled comfortably.

"Kumo, we have talked before. We talk again. I offered you friendship. Are you ready to accept it?"

Kumo's eyes were full of sullen anger.

"No. You take everything, you give nothing. That is not friendship."

"I told you I would make you chief of all the valleys."

Kumo's head came up, defiantly.

"Already I am chief of the valleys."

Sonderfeld laughed in his face.

"There is a luluai in every village appointed by the Kiap in Goroka. These are the chiefs. You are still a work-boy, eating the offal of the lowly."

Kumo grinned with cunning and contempt.

"The luluais do as I tell them. But you are still the servant of the Kiap. How can you do for me what you cannot do for yourself?"

Sonderfeld shook his head.

"You do not believe that, otherwise you would not have told the tribes of the coming of the Red Spirit. I am no man's servant. I am the Red Spirit, who is the Ruler of all – of the Kiaps and of the Pig God himself."

Kumo squirted a stream of betel juice at a passing lizard.

"You say so. But you do not speak in the councils of the Kiaps. Among the tribes you do no magic."

"Because I am not yet ready?"

Now it was Kumo's turn to laugh, a deep throaty chuckle that welled and gurgled behind his scarlet teeth. Sonderfeld flicked up the cane and struck him viciously on the cheek, raising a long, thin weal from mouth to ear. Kumo yelped and clapped his hands to his face.

"Now," said Sonderfeld calmly, "you will listen to me."

The sorcerer glared at him in helpless fury.

"You are a fool, Kumo. But I am prepared to forget your folly and make you my friend."

"No! You are not my friend. Does a brother strike his brother? The Kiap's law says the white man shall not strike the black man. I shall tell the Kiap and you will be punished."

Sonderfeld shrugged and spread his hands in a gesture of indifference.

"Tell the Kiap. But first listen to me."

"No."

He turned and made as if to go. Sonderfeld's next words stopped him dead in his tracks.

"Last night, after the carry-leg, you lay with a woman in the grass."

Slowly, fearfully, Kumo turned to face him. Sonderfeld grinned in mockery.

"When the elders made you a man, Kumo, did they not tell you that he who puts his seed to a strange woman puts his life in great danger?"

"This was no stranger. She was a woman of my village."

The words were defiant, but there was uncertainty in his voice.

"The woman was my woman," said Sonderfeld calmly. "Her name is N'Daria. She serves the Red Spirit."

A gleam of confidence showed in the red, sullen eyes of Kumo. He remembered the protestations of the girl, her passion and her desire for him.

"Does the Red Spirit share his women then?"

"No. He does not share them. He uses them to do his work. Look!"

The bamboo tube was in his hand. He thrust it under the nose of the sorcerer. Kumo drew back startled and puzzled.

"What is that?"

Sonderfeld's voice rose to hieratic thunder.

"You lay with a woman, Kumo. Your spittle was on her lips and your blood was under the nails of her fingers

. . . and you lay with her. I hold your life in my hands before you."

Kumo's reaction was sudden and horrible.

His spine arched backwards, his head fell back. His eyes rolled upward. A bubbling imbecile sound broke from his lips. Then, as if he had been kicked in the belly, he doubled forward, retched and crumpled, trembling and gibbering, at Sonderfeld's feet.

Sonderfeld was startled, but only for a moment. Then he smiled, looked down at the twitching body, and knew with absolute certainty that he had only to walk away and the sorcerer would crawl to the nearest bush and lie there, without food or water or speech, until he died. Kumo had killed others in the same way. Now the sword of the spirit, the terrible two-edged weapon of fear and belief had been turned against his own unarmoured flesh.

For Sonderfeld it was a moment of pure triumph. Alone he had joined battle with the dark and secret rulers of the valleys. The evidence of his victory lay dusty and abject at his feet. He stooped and hauled Kumo upright by his thick, greasy hair. Then he propped him against a tree and stood, arms akimbo, mocking him.

"Now do you believe me, Kumo?"

"Yes." It was a drunken nod.

"You know that I am the Red Spirit with life or death in my hands?"

"Yes."

"You know that I can burn you with fire, or crush you with stones, or have the ants devour you even as you walk?"

The sorcerer's face twisted in hypnotic agonies.

"Yes . . . yes . . . yes."

"You know also that I can preserve your life if I wish it?"

Kumo opened his eyes. There was no hope in them, only an animal pleading.

"I know."

"If you serve me, I will preserve it."

"I will serve."

"If you serve me well, then one day, perhaps, I will give it back to you."

Kumo tried to speak, but no words came from his slack and babbling mouth. The impact of even this small hope robbed him of human speech. Satisfied with his little comedy of cruelty, Sonderfeld walked up to him and slapped him hard on both cheeks.

"Stand up !"

Kumo stood up.

"Your life is safe, so long as you do as you are told."

Kumo nodded vigorously, still without the power of speech.

"Now," said Sonderfeld quietly. "you will listen to me. You are a great sorcerer. You understand how a man may be killed so than none can tell who struck him?"

Kumo found tongue at last.

"I understand."

"Good. There is a man in my house whom you know. He is the one who lives in the village and sits with you by the cook-fires and asks questions of the women."

"I know him."

"Today he goes back to his own house in the village. Tonight you will kill him – but so that the Kiap Curtis will think he died in his bed. Can you do that?"

The man's eagerness was horrible.

"I can do it. There is a powerful magic that –"

Sonderfeld cut him off with a gesture.

"I do not want to hear. Do it and tell no one. Come to me when I send for you but not before – and Kumo –" His voice was a silken thread. "When the Red Spirit appears at the pig festival, will you proclaim him to the tribes?"

"I will proclaim him."

"Good," said Kurt Sonderfeld in his own tongue. "Good and good and – *wundershön* !"

He threw back his head and laughed and laughed while the birds rose fluttering and squawking from the thicket, and Kumo the Sorcerer watched him with the fear of death in his heart.

Down in the Kiap house, Patrol Officer Curtis was groaning in the grip of a hangover. His head throbbed, his eyes were full of gravel, and his mouth was parched and foul. His stomach heaved at the first taste of the bitter tea brought to him by the police-boy.

Theodore Nelson scooped the sugary pulp from a paw-paw and grinned at him across the yellow rind.

"Try some of this, my dear chap. Cleans the palate, settles the digestion. Wonderful stuff."

"Go to hell!"

"Drink your tea then. You're as dry as a chip. You won't feel better till you get some liquid inside you."

Curtis groaned and gagged over another mouthful.

"Dunno why I drink whisky. It always hits me like this."

"It was a very good whisky." Nelson chewed happily on the soft fruit. "I'll say this for Sonderfeld, he's a perfect host."

"I think he's an arrogant swine."

Curtis buried his nose in the tin pannikin while Nelson studied him with shrewd and twinkling eyes. There was truth in whisky, and it was one of his subtler pleasures to pry out the truth in other people's lives and savour its folly or its tragedy without involving his own transient person.

"Arrogant, yes. But a swine? You know him better than I do, of course."

Curtis rose like a trout to a well-cast fly.

"Any man who treats a woman the way Sonderfeld treats his wife is a swine for my money."

Nelson hid his smile with another spoonful of fruit. He nodded gravely. His eyes were full of sympathy for the bruised and knightly spirit of youth. Curtis took

67

another mouthful of tea and wiped his lips with a stained handkerchief.

"Sonderfeld's as cold as a fish. Gerda's a warm person, full of life, hungry for affection."

"I gathered she was getting at least half a meal," said Nelson dryly.

Curtis's chin came up defiantly.

"What do you mean?"

"Lansing's the man of the moment, isn't he?"

For a moment Nelson thought the boy was going to strike him, then quite suddenly the anger went out of him, his face crumpled childishly, his eyes filled with tears of self-pity.

"I suppose he is. But I don't blame Gerda. She's alone up here. Lansing's close and – well, I don't begrudge her what she gets from him."

"Why should it matter to you one way or the other?"

There was a queer pathetic dignity about him as he raised his head and looked Nelson full in the eyes.

"Because I'm in love with her myself."

Theodore Nelson sat transfixed, the spoon half-way to his mouth, the great yellow fruit held precariously on his open palm. The blunt admission shocked him. A mild flirtation, a casual accommodation, would have amused him, but the grand passion was a different matter altogether.

"God Almighty!" he swore softly. "You are in a mess, aren't you?"

Curtis nodded, miserably.

"That's why I got drunk last night. Never touch the stuff usually. Can't afford to when I'm on the round. Never know when you're liable to wake up with an arrow in your guts or a hatchet in your skull. But . . . to sit there at the table with her. To hear her laugh. To know that when we were gone she'd. . . ."

He buried his face in his hands as if to shut out a tormenting vision.

Nelson scooped out the last mouthfuls of fruit, laid

68

the empty skin on the floor of the hut, wiped his hands, and lit a cigarette. Then he stood up.

"It's none of my business, of course, but if you'd take a word of advice from an old stager –"

"Yes?" Curtis raised his head slowly.

"Get out of the valley today. Finish the patrol, go back to Goroka, and ask for a transfer to another area. If you don't, you're going to be in trouble – up to the neck."

"You think I don't know that?"

Nelson looked down at the boy's face, yellow with hangover, ravaged by the grief and torment of young passion. Pity touched him rarely, but he felt it now – pity and scorn and distaste for the folly from which his own cautious nature had preserved him.

"If you know it, why stay?"

"Because there's trouble brewing and it's my job to find out what it is and put a stop to it."

My God, thought Nelson, there's the makings of a man in him. He's flabby with puppy-fat still, but there's a sound, stiff core underneath.

"Trouble? You said last night there was no trouble. You laughed at Lansing and that little parson fellow."

"I was drunk last night," said Curtis slowly. "I made a fool of myself in more ways than one. But I sobered up after I was sick. I lay awake for hours thinking about it, trying to fit things together."

"What did you make of it?"

"Nothing definite – except that Sonderfeld's involved. That means Gerda's involved too. I'm going to stay around for a few days, visit a few of the other villages, and see what information I can pick up."

"From whom?"

"From the luluais, from the tribal gossip and ..." He hesitated a moment. "... From Lansing and Père Louis."

Nelson grinned, savouring the irony of the situation.

"I thought you didn't like either of 'em."

Curtis frowned.

"I don't. But this is Administration business. My love life doesn't come into it, nor my religion. Lansing's got information that I want. The missioners live closer to the tribes than any other people in the Territory – especially the R.Cs. because they don't marry and they have to share the tribal life or live like hermits."

"Why don't you like the missionaries?"

Curtis shrugged.

"We're not ready for 'em. Make a man a Christian and you tell him that all men are brothers in Christ. His next question is why can't I sit at a table with my brothers and marry the white women and say my piece in the Kiap councils and earn the same money as a white worker. It's too early for that – half a century too early."

Nelson was puzzled. This was no longer the braying youth of last night's dinner party. This was a sober young official who knew his job and was prepared to do it at some cost to himself and some damage to his heartstrings. Give him confidence and polish, teach him the art of silence among his elders, the boy would make a good administrator – provided Delilah didn't shear him of his strength and bed him down to messy marital scandal.

The boy's face broke into a rueful smile.

"Don't worry, Nelson. I'll get you back to Goroka in one piece. Take it easy and enjoy yourself. You'll probably find it very interesting."

"I wasn't thinking of myself," said Nelson soberly. "I was thinking of you."

Curtis's eyes darkened.

"You mind your business. I'll mind mine."

"And Mrs. Sonderfeld's?"

"Go to hell!"

He stalked out of the hut and Nelson heard him shouting angrily to the police-boys. When he looked out the doorway he saw Curtis standing naked in the bright

70

sun while a pair of grinning fuzzy-wuzzies doused him
with water from canvas buckets. His skin was shining.
His muscles rippled as he gasped and danced and swung
his arms. His belly was flat and hard as a board.

Nelson was filled with sour admiration for his youth
and his vitality and his resilient, glowing strength. He
wondered what would happen if Gerda Sonderfeld
should fall in love with them.

CHAPTER 6

IN the warmth of the rich mountain morning, Max Lansing walked home to his village. It lay in a deep saucer-
shaped depression between Père Louis' community and
the Lahgi Valley. To reach it, he had to make a wide
traverse westward of Sonderfeld's property and cross
two steep saddles before he struck the path that led over
the lip of the crater and downward into the taro plots
and the banana groves and the dancing park. He would
not reach it till the middle of the afternoon.

He had a water-bottle hooked to his belt and a canvas
knapsack filled with food from Gerda's kitchen and a
bottle of Sonderfeld's best whisky. By midday he would
have crossed the first saddle and he would rest and eat
by the swift water that came singing down over the
rocks from the high peaks. Then he would push on, with
neither joy nor impatience, to the small bamboo hut on
the outer edge of the village – his home for the years of
his subsidized exile.

As he topped the rise that overlooked the plantation,
he halted a moment and looked back. He saw the blaze
of Gerda's garden, the nestling of the bungalow under its
thatched roof, the long serried lines of the plantation
trees. He saw the work-boys moving about like leisurely
ants and the white tall figure of Sonderfeld standing at
the head of the first grove. He saw them all as a symbol

71

of permanence and possession, a mockery of his own rootless, pointless existence.

Long, long ago he had been fired with zeal for knowledge – knowledge for its own sake, knowledge without thought of gain, profitless except in human dignity and spiritual enlargement. But the fire had burnt out years since and he saw himself, not great among the solitary great ones, but a poor and tattered pedant, piling his dry facts like children's blocks, while the laughing, weeping, lusting, suffering world rolled heedless past his doorstep. Without faith in himself and in his work, he found himself without strength for dedication. He could no longer walk happy among the scholars, and he had forgotten the speech of the market-place. Even his love was a pedantry, dusty and dry beside the welling passion of Gerda.

When Sonderfeld had left the house, he had sat with her at breakfast on the veranda and he had tried to recapture the brief warmth of their night's embrace. But Gerda refused to match his mood. She had talked, cheerfully enough, about the dinner party, the guests, the plantation, the news from Goroka. But when he had urged her to discussion of their own relationship, she had refused, gently but with finality.

"No, Max. All that can be put into words has been said between us. I am here, whenever you care to come. I will be with you as I have always been. But I will not talk – talk – talk! Better to kiss or make love, or simply walk among the flowers together. But why rake our hearts with words that mean nothing?"

To which, of course, there was no answer. Take it or leave it. He had not courage to leave it and he lacked the wisdom to take without question. He must itch and scratch and itch and scratch again, until the warm and willing heart was scarred into a running sore.

He had risen abruptly from the table and gathered his things to leave. She had come to him then and kissed him with that maddening maternal gentleness.

"Don't be angry with me, Max. I am as I am. I cannot change. But before you go, let me tell you one thing."

"Yes?"

Let her tell him she loved him and he would be happy again. Let her give him one small hope and ambition would soar again, mountains high.

"Be careful, Max, I beg of you. Be careful!"

"Careful of what?"

Her hands made a helpless, fluttering gesture.

"I don't know. I wish I did. But after what you said last night, my husband —"

"To hell with your husband!"

He caught her to him, crushing his mouth brutally on hers. Then he released her, picked up his knapsack and without a backward glance strode off, a lost and angry man, storming up the hillside.

When he came to the river he was sweating and exhausted. It was a long walk at the best of times, but for a lonely and unhappy fellow, it was twice as tedious. He plunged down to the water, and felt the humid air close round him like a curtain. A cloud of insects enveloped him. He beat at them irritably with his handkerchief and by the time he reached the sandy hollow near the ford he was free of them.

He slipped off his knapsack, took a long pull at the water-bottle and flung himself down at the edge of the clear-singing water. He was too tired to eat, so he lay sprawled on his back, head pillowed on the knapsack, looking up into the dappled green of the jungle overhang, through a cloud of bright blue butterflies. He saw the flash of brilliant scarlet as a Bird of Paradise made his mating dance on the branch of an albizzia tree. A tiny tree kangaroo peered cautiously between two broad purple leaves. A lizard sunned himself on the rock beside him, and in the undergrowth he heard the scurrying of small animals, rooting for food.

The thought struck him that in his four-hour walk he had seen not a single human being. This was unusual, for the mountain paths were the highways of the tribes. Since the white man's law had abolished war and killing raids, there was a modest traffic between the villages in canes and Birds of Paradise feathers had gum and galip nuts and pigs and the produce of the gardens.

This traffic had been increased of late by the movement of the tribes for the approaching pig festival. Yet today he had seen no one. Because he was tired, the thought nagged at him uneasily. He fumbled for a cigarette, lit it and watched the blue smoke spiral up towards the green canopy.

Then he heard it, distant but distinct – chuff-chuff-chuff – the unmistakable beat of a running cassowary. The sound was unusual enough to interest him. The cassowary bird was native to the high valleys, but the breed was being thinned out by killing and the survivors were retreating into the less populated mountains.

The footsteps came closer, thudding like the muffled beat of a train on steel rails. Lansing sat up. The bird was coming down the same path that he had followed. He wondered if it would break out on to the beach. He was not afraid, only interested. The big, ungainly bird was easily frightened and would not attack a human being unless it was angered or cornered. The footsteps came closer and closer. Then they stopped.

He judged the bird was probably a dozen yards away, hidden by the dense screen of undergrowth. He could hear its rustling among the leaves and low branches. Then the rustling stopped, and after a moment Lansing lay back drowsily against the knapsack. He thought he would sleep a little, then eat before he continued his walk. He worked a hollow for his hip in the warm sand and turned comfortably on his side.

Then he saw it.

A yard from his face was a small white snake, dappled with black spots. In the suspended moment of shock he saw the trail of its body in the white sand. It had come from the bush at his back, the deadliest reptile

74

in the whole island. If it struck him, he would die, paralysed and beyond help within two hours. Cautiously, he moved his hand to get purchase on the sand, then, with a single movement, he thrust himself to his feet. In that same moment the snake moved, fast as a flicker of light to the spot where his head and lain. Its jaws opened and it struck at the stiff canvas of the knapsack. Before Lansing had time to snatch up a stick or stone it was gone again, a dappled death, slithering into the fallen leaves at the fringe of the bush.

Sick with terror, he stood looking down at the knapsack and the tiny dark stain of the ejected poison. Then he shivered, snatched up the bag, and plunged across the ford, heedless of the water that swirled about his knees and hidden stones that sent him half-sprawling into the icy current.

Gerda's parting words beat in his brain.

"Be careful, Max, I beg of you. Be careful!"

Breathless, he scrambled up the steep bank and looked back at the small white beach. It was bare and empty of life. The jungle was like a painted back-drop, motionless in the heavy air.

Then, he heard it again – chuff-chuff-chuff – the running feet of the cassowary, retreating into the stillness.

Suddenly he remembered. The cassowary men! They were an old story in the valleys, an old fear among the tribes. They were sorcerers who, by common repute, had power to change themselves into cassowary birds and run faster than the wind. They were the Territory counterpart of the Carpathian werewolves and the jackal-men of Africa. The tribes believed in them implicitly and for proof pointed to the claw marks on the soft ground after a nocturnal visit from one of the sorcerers. New-comers to the mountains scoffed at such rank super-stition, but the old hands – traders, missionaries, senior men in the district services – were less sceptical. Each had his own stories to tell of phenomena apparently beyond physical explanation. But all had one thing in common, a healthy respect and a prickling fear of the dim borderlands of primitive mysticism.

Lansing himself had at first rejected the manifestations as pure charlatanry. But the more he studied, the less certain he became; and now, in the eerie solitude of the upland paths, he, too, was gripped by the cold, uncanny fear of the bird-man.

It was late in the afternoon when he came to the village. The mountain shadows were lengthening and the first faint chill was creeping down the valley. He was hungry and tired and trembling as if with the onset of fever. He paid no heed to the curious stares of the villagers, but went straight to his hut, crammed a couple of suppressant tablets in his mouth, stripped himself naked and sponged himself with water from the canvas bucket.

When he was clean and dressed in fresh clothes, he poured himself a noggin of Sonderfeld's whisky and tossed it off at a gulp. He poured another, tempered it with water, and stood in his doorway with the glass in his hand, looking out on the village.

The women were coming up from the taro gardens, naked except for the pubic belt, their thick bodies bowed under the weight of string baskets full of sweet potatoes which they carried suspended from their broad foreheads and supported on the small of their backs. In the far corner of the compound a young girl was feeding the pigs. They were blinded so that they could not run away, and tethered to stakes of casuarina wood. They grunted and snuffled and squealed as she passed among them with fruit rinds and bananas and taro pulp.

The pigs and the gardens and the children, these were the charges of the women – and in that order. A woman would suckle a child at one breast and a piglet at the other. The men would make the gardens, laying them out, breaking the first soil, marking each patch with the small blunt mound of the phallic symbol crossed with the cut that represented the female principle. But it was the women who tilled them and dug the big ripe tubers that were the staple diet of the tribe.

As for the men, they sat as they sat now, one making a ceremonial wig of fibre and gum and flaring feathers and green beetle-shards, another plaiting a cane socket for his obsidian axe, this one chipping a round stone for the head of his club, that one stringing the short cane bow which would bring down birds and possums and the furry cuscus whose tail made armlets for the bucks and the unmarried girls.

Looking at them there, bent over their small tasks, Lansing thought how like children they were, intent, mistrustful, jealous of their trivial possessions. The second thought came hard on the heels of the first. They were not children. They were adults, intelligent within the limits of their knowledge, bound by sanctions older than the Pentateuch, preoccupied with the problems of birth, death – and survival for the years between.

To the outsider their tasks were trivial, but in the small stringent world of the tribal unit they were of major importance. Let a blight come on the taro patch, the whole village must move to new territory. If the pigs should be stricken with swine fever, they would have no protein in their diet – the ancient island of New Guinea is poor in all but the smallest animal life.

They went naked because there were no furs to give them warmth. They practised abortion and birth-control because there was a limit to the crops that could be raised in the narrow gardens, and because the pigs were decimated at festival after festival by a meat-hungry people, bound, moreover, by the primal need to propitiate a hostile Pig God in whom lay the principle of fertility. They had no written language. They had never made a wheel. Their traditions were buried in ancient words and phrases that even the elders could not translate.

In their narrow, uncertain world, love, as the white man knew it, did not exist. The girl who made the love-play in the kunande would be raped on her wedding night and her husband would scowl if she wore any but the simplest ornament. In certain villages a man chose his bride by firing an arrow in her thigh – an act of hostility and enslavement.

In this climate of fear, behind the closed frontiers of the razorbacks, superstition flourished like a rank growth and the old magical practices of the dawn people were the straws to which the simple clung for security and the clubs which the ambitious used to bludgeon them into submission.

As he sipped his whisky and watched the small but complex pattern unfold itself, Lansing was conscious of his own inadequacy. Two years now he had lived among these people. His note-books were full of careful observations on every aspect of their life-pattern, yet he was as far from understanding them as he had been on the day of his arrival. It was as if there were a curtain drawn between him and the arcana of their secret life, and unless he could penetrate the curtain, his work would be without significance.

The missionaries did better. The old ones, like Père Louis, did best of all. They came unabashed to make commerce in souls and spirits. They had secrets of their own to trade. They offered protection against the sorcerers, an answer to the ambient mystery of creation.

But when you didn't believe in the soul, when you were committed by birth and training to the pragmatic materialism of the twentieth century, what then? You were shut out from the sanctuary, condemned to walk in the Courts of the Strangers, denied access to the mysteries and the sacrifice.

He tossed off the dregs of his whisky, rinsed the glass carefully and set it on the table. Then he walked out into the compound.

There was a girl in the village whom he had trained to look after him, to wash his clothes and tidy his hut and prepare his food with moderate cleanliness. He had not seen her since his arrival; he was going to look for her.

First, he went to her father's hut. The girl was not there. The old man was sitting outside the door sharpening a set of cane arrows. When Lansing questioned him, he gave him a sidelong look, shrugged indifferently, and bent over his work. Accustomed to the moodiness of the mountain folk, Lansing made no comment but walked over to a group of women bending over a fire-pit.

They giggled and simpered and exchanged smiles of secret amusement, but they would tell him nothing. He was irritated, but he dared not show it for fear of losing face. He hailed the women coming up from the taro gardens. They shook their heads. They had not set eyes on the girl. He tried the children, but they drew away from him and ran to hide their faces behind the buttocks of their mothers.

Then, suddenly, he became aware that the whole village was watching him. They had not paused for a moment in their work, but they were following his every movement, eyes slanting and secret, their smiles a silent mockery. They were not hostile, they were simply amused. They were watching a dancing doll, jerked this way and that by forces beyond his control.

Anger rose in him, sour and acid from the pit of his belly. He wanted to shout at them, curse them, strike them at least into recognition of his presence. He knew he could not do it. The loss of face would be final and irrecoverable.

He turned on his heel and with elaborate slowness walked back to his hut. He closed the door and lit the lamp. His hands were trembling and his palms were clammy with sweat. This concerted mockery was new in his experience. Sullenness he had met and had learnt to ignore. Suspicion had been rasped and honed away by the daily, familiar intercourse. This was something different. It was like ... he fumbled for a tag to identify the strangeness ... like being sent to Coventry. But for what?

He knew enough of ritual and custom to make him careful of their observance. He had crossed no one of the elders. He was aloof from village scandal. There was no reason why they should turn against him. Then he thought of Sonderfeld and of Kumo and of Gerda's cryptic warning, and he was suddenly afraid.

He thought of Père Louis and the dappled snake and the sound of the unseen cassowary bird, and his fear was a wild, screaming terror. He was alone and naked and defenceless among the secret people in the darkening valley.

Desperately he struggled for control. At all costs he must show a brave face to the village mockery, must maintain the simple order of his studious existence.

He broke out Gerda's package of food and tried to eat. The cold food gagged him and he thrust it away. He lit the spirit lamp and tried to work over his notes, but the letters danced confusedly before his eyes and his trembling fingers could not control the pencil.

Then, with the abrupt coming of darkness, the kundus began their maddening climactic rhythm. He felt as though they were throbbing inside his skull-case, thudding and pounding till his brain must burst into wild, incurable madness.

Then he knew what he must do if he were to get through the night. He set the whisky bottle and the water canteen on the table in front of him, broke out a fresh packet of cigarettes, pushed the lamp to a safe distance from his elbow, and began carefully and methodically to get himself drunk.

He drank slowly at first lest his empty stomach revolt and cheat him of relief. Then, as the liquor warmed and relaxed him, he poured larger tots and used less water, until finally he was drinking neat spirit and the level of the bottle was below the half-way mark.

Long before the drums were silent, long before the

singers were dumb, Max Lansing was slumped across his table, with his head pillowed on his unfinished manuscript, one nerveless hand lying on an overturned bottle, the other dangling over a broken glass and a pool of liquor that soaked slowly into the earthen floor.

Then Kumo came in.

All through the solitary orgy he had been squatting outside the hut watching Lansing's slow collapse into insensibility. He was dressed in the ceremonial costume with the tossing plumes and the clattering ornaments of pearlshell. His long, crescent nose ornament gave him the air of a tusked animal. Tucked in his fur armband he carried a small, closed tube of bamboo.

For a long moment he stood over the unconscious man, then with a sudden gesture he lifted his head by the hair and let it fall with a thump on the table. Lansing made no sound. His head lolled into equilibrium on one cheek and one ear. Kumo grunted with satisfaction, and took the bamboo tube in his hands.

First he rolled it rapidly between his fingers, then tapped it rapidly on the edge of the desk, making a dry, drumming sound. Finally, he held it a long time against the hot glass of the lamp, so that the warmth soaked through the pithy wood and into the hollow centre.

Now he was ready.

Carefully he took up his position between the edge of the table and the open door of the hut. Then he bent over Lansing, holding the butt of the tube in one hand, in the other its cap – pointing downwards, six inches from Lansing's face. With a sharp movement, he pulled off the cap and stepped backwards. There was a soft "plop" and a small, dappled snake fell on to the desk.

Maddened by the noise and the movement and the heat, the snake struck and struck again at Lansing's cheek. Then it slithered off the table and disappeared in the shadows of the hut.

Anaesthetized by the liquor, Lansing felt no pain and

made no movement. Kumo stood a moment looking down at his victim and at the twin punctures just below his cheekbone. Then, silently as the snake, he, too, went out into the darkness and soon, over the beat of the drums, the villagers heard the thudding feet of the cassowary bird.

CHAPTER 7

A RUNNER from Lansing's village brought the news to Patrol Officer Lee Curtis as he sat taking the census outside the Kiap house. He had come, loping steadily over the mountain trails, and he arrived sweating and breathless to pour out, with oratorical flourish, the carefully rehearsed message from the luluai.

The white man was dead. The whole village grieved for the loss of their brother. Except that the Kiap disapproved, they would chop off their finger joints in the old fashion of mourning. The white man was dead, struck down by a snake while he slept thus over his table. The marks of the snake were here and here on his face. There was a girl who served him his food. She had discovered him when she came to his hut early in the morning. The white man had been drinking. There was water and a bottle of yellow spirit thus and thus on the table. The snake had come and gone and the white man had not stirred. If the Kiap wished, the villagers would smoke the body for him and send it over the mountain. Otherwise he should come and fetch it quickly; if not, it would stink very soon. The white man was dead and the luluai had given orders that none should touch him until word came from the Kiap. The door of his hut was closed and the white man still as they found him, waiting for the Kiap to come.

There was more and more yet, as the courier, drunk with his own eloquence, embellished the tale for the Kiap and the police-boys and the circle of awe-struck villagers. Yet, stripped of its primitive rhetoric, it was a good story, well told. All the facts were there, the setting was sharply and accurately sketched. The pivotal incident – that of the striking snake – was more than feasible. Reptiles abound in the high valleys. They are as much at home in the thatched villages as they are in the kunai grass. Most of them are deadly poisonous.

Yet Lee Curtis was not satisfied. Young as he was, he had been well trained, first in the School of Pacific Administration, then under the watchful eye and the rasping tongue of George Oliver, A.D.O., at Goroka. And the theme dinned and drummed into him every day and all day was: Mistrust the simple and the straight-forward. The native mind deals in subtleties and inversions and complexities not always apparent to the white man.

This story was too simple, too bland and pat, too careful and too accurate to be the whole truth.

When the runner had finished his peroration, Curtis sat a long time in silence watching him. He asked no questions. The answers would have told him nothing. The man was a mouthpiece who would say what he had been told to say, and after that would relapse into blank stupidity. Under the wordless scrutiny, the runner began to be uneasy. He glanced about him furtively to see only the stony stares of the coastal police-boys and the gaping curiosity of the mountain folk. He hung his head and scuffed his toes in the dust.

Curtis stood up. He snapped an order to the sergeant to continue with the census and see that none of the villagers left the Kiap hut until he came back. He would have the boys ready to march within the hour.

The fuzzy-haired sergeant saluted smartly and took his place at the table, while Curtis walked slowly up the path in the direction of Sonderfeld's plantation.

On the face of it, his duty was simple. He would go out to the mountain village. He would confirm that Lansing had died of snake-bite. He would bury him with simple ceremony. He would pack his notes and his belongings, and send them with an inventory to the A.D.O. at Goroka. He would file a report of his findings and his procedures – and the case would be closed. No problems, no complications, no personal involvement for a young official with his way still to make in the world.

Even as he thought it, he knew that he could not do it. The talk of the night before, Lansing's blunt comment on the restlessness of the tribes, the undercurrent of tension between Sonderfeld and the missionary and Lansing himself, still nagged at him like an aching tooth. Behind these three was Gerda, the woman he loved, the woman whose lover was dead. And behind these again, in the background of bright mountains and dark valleys, was the shadowy figure of Kumo the Sorcerer. Before he could close the case he must know more of these people and their relationship one to another. He must investigate without appearing to do so. He must presume a crime where the evidence said there was no crime. He must have constantly in mind the uneasy position of the Trustee Administration responsible to the United Nations, sensitive to "incidents" that might make headlines in the world Press.

Half-way up the path he stopped to light a cigarette. From this point, he could command a view of the house and of the plantation itself. He saw that Sonderfeld and Nelson and Wee Georgie were half a mile away studying the drainage problems of the new clearing. His first impulse was to go to them and tell them the news. Then he looked up at the bungalow. Gerda would be there – alone. She had a right to hear the news from someone who felt for her. Perhaps, in the first shock, she would give him something on which to ground his dangerous investigation.

Again he looked across at the plantation and saw Sonderfeld and his companions moving farther away from the house. He had twenty minutes at least. With a gesture of decision he tossed away the half-smoked cigarette and walked swiftly up to the bungalow.

Gerda was in the summer-house among the orchid blooms. She wore sandals and a frock of flowered cotton and a wide, straw hat caught under her chin with a bow of ribbon. She looked up when he entered, smiled with pleasure and surprise, pulled off her stained gloves, and stretched out her hands in greeting.

"Dear Mr. Curtis! This is a nice surprise. You must have known I was lonely."

He took her hands and, moved by a sudden boyish impulse, raised them to his lips.

The gesture seemed to make her uneasy. When he released her she stepped back a little and leant against one of the shelves that held the orchid pots. She was still smiling, but there was puzzlement in her eyes and a small flush crept upwards under her ivory skin.

For a long moment Curtis stood irresolute, eyes downcast, searching for the words to frame his message. Then he raised his head. His voice was unsteady.

"I – I'm afraid I've brought you bad news."

She stiffened. Her eyes widened, her lips parted. The words came in a faltering whisper.

"Bad news? I don't understand."

"Max Lansing died last night. Snake-bite. A runner brought me the news ten minutes ago."

She did not cry out. She did not weep. But her whole body was rigid and her eyes were staring with blank horror. She held tightly to the rough wood of the shelf, arching her back against it.

Lee Curtis stood helpless, incapable of even a small gesture of comfort. Gerda shuddered and buried her face in her hands. He laid a tentative hand on her dark hair. She jerked away.

"No! No! Don't touch me."

He drew back and watched her recover herself, slowly and painfully. Then at last, she faced him, dry-eyed, tight-lipped. The horror was gone from her eyes. Now, they were blazing with hate. Her voice was tight, but steady and full of challenge.

"Mr. Curtis !"

"Yes?"

"Mr. Curtis, you are the representative of the Administration."

"That's right."

"You have police powers as well?"

"In this area – yes."

"Then –" She looked him full in the eyes. Her voice was cold as stone. "Then I want to tell you that Max Lansing was murdered – by my husband."

The blunt accusation shocked him like a douche of cold water. He spoke carefully.

"Lansing died some time last night in a village fifteen miles from here. Your husband did not leave the plantation."

"I know that. He did not need to. He arranged for Max to be killed by Kumo the Sorcerer."

"Can you prove that?"

"No. But I believe it to be true."

"Why?"

"Because of what was said last night. Max made it plain that he believed Kurt was implicated in the trouble among the tribes."

"There is no trouble yet –"

Her anger blazed out at him.

"No, but there will be – and why? Because you and your kind will not listen to the men who know – like Max and Père Louis. You come up here with your police-boys and your guns and your little book. You make a great show and then you go away – and all the time Kurt and Kumo and the rest have been laughing at you, throwing dust in your eyes."

Breathless with anger, she stood fronting him, battering on the light armour of his youthful self-control. Before he had time to answer her she returned to the attack.

"And now a man is dead. A snake bit him. The verdict? Accident – act of God – death by misadventure ! ! It is murder, I tell you. Murder ! And the man who planned it is Kurt, my husband, who is so filled with his own pride that he imagines himself Lord of All, Master of Life and Death – like the Red Spirit."

Then, without warning, she wept. Her body was shaken with great sobs and she buried her ravaged face in her white hands. This time, he reached out and drew her to him and held her, unresisting, pressed against his breast until the spasm passed and she was crying quietly.

She drew away from him at last and lifted her face again. Hands and lips and eyes were eloquent in the broken appeal.

"What do I have to do? What more do I have to say to make you believe me?"

"I believe you, Gerda," said Lee Curtis softly.

"You do?" There was wonderment and gratitude in her eyes.

He nodded.

"I believe you, because I love you."

"Oh, no !" It was a cry of pure anguish. She cringed away from him as if he had struck her. "Not you, too. Please leave me alone. I'm tired. I have my own life to live. I cannot bear the burden of yours as well."

Lee Curtis was hurt and troubled, but he had delicacy enough to apologize.

"I'm sorry. I shouldn't have said that. I – I promise not to bother you. Really I won't. I understand what you're telling me. I believe you may be right. But you must understand I can't move. I can't give even a hint of suspicion until I have evidence. Solid evidence. You see that, don't you?"

She nodded wearily.

"I do. I'll try to get it. I don't know how, but I'll try. Meantime, have you told my husband?"

"No. I thought it would be kinder to tell you first."

She reached up and patted his cheek with the same vague, tender gesture that had irritated Max Lansing.

"You're a good, kind, young man. I'm sorry I made a scene."

Curtis stiffened. Mention of his youth brought back all his uneasiness and his sense of isolation. He spoke crisply, officially, to cover his embarrassment.

"If you can carry it off, I'd rather you didn't let your husband know I've seen you. He's in the plantation. I'm going to tell him now."

Gerda nodded.

"I can carry it off, as you say."

"Good. Find out whatever you can and let me know. But ..." He hesitated, then the words came out with a rush. "For God's sake be careful, Gerda. Be very, very careful."

"I'll be careful. I promise."

But he did not hear her. He was already gone, a shamefaced, troubled, scared young man striding through the dappled sunlight to see Kurt Sonderfeld.

Sonderfeld professed himself deeply shocked by the news. He swore softly in German and beat his forehead with his fist.

"The poor fellow! The poor, poor fellow! Gerda will be upset. I am myself. He was angry with me, I think. He left without saying good-bye. Now he is dead and we have no time to be friends again. He was drunk, you say?"

Curtis nodded.

"Sounds like it from the reports."

"Natural enough. He would be lonely when he got back. He would drink to put himself early to sleep. That is the curse of this life – the isolation, the black depression. I know. I have felt it myself."

Wee Georgie whistled softly. His beady, bloodshot eyes were bright with interest.

"Snakes, eh? Makes you think don't it? Place is alive

88

with the bloody things and yet a man walks about all day in bare feet, sleeps six inches from the floor. Strewth!"

Theodore Nelson clucked his sympathy. He had travelled too much and too comfortably to be moved by Lansing's untimely death. He was more interested in Lee Curtis. The boy knew more than he was telling. He was unhappy about something, scared, too, probably, but he was putting up a good front. His hands were steady and his eyes were cold, and there was a reassuring firmness in the set of his downy chin.

"If there is anything I can do – ?" said Sonderfeld, tentatively.

"There is – yes." Curtis's voice was crisp with authority. "I'm going up to the village this afternoon. I'll have to inspect the body, arrange for the burial, collect Lansing's things, make a report. I'd like you to come with me."

Sonderfeld could not conceal his surprise.

"If you say so, of course. But I do not see what good I can do."

"You're a doctor," said Curtis bluntly. "I need a death certificate. I may need a post-mortem. You're entitled to refuse, of course."

"My dear fellow!" The big man was bland and smiling. "I wouldn't dream of refusing. The Administration has been good to me. I am happy to serve the Administration. When do you want to leave?"

"In half an hour. Even at that, we'll be walking in the dark."

Sonderfeld shrugged.

"I shall be ready. Now, if you'll excuse me, gentlemen, I should like a few minutes with my wife. She was very – attached to our friend, Lansing. Come, Georgie!"

He strode off over the soft, black earth with the fat man shuffling and wheezing at his heels like a decrepit spaniel. Nelson and Curtis were left alone in the clearing.

"Cigarette?" said Nelson gently.

"Thanks."

They lit up. Curtis was still staring across the plantation at the retreating figure of Sonderfeld.

"Trouble, Curtis?"

"Part of the job."

Nelson grinned at the cryptic reply. He was a hard man to snub.

"That doesn't answer my question."

Curtis slewed round to face him. His patience was wearing thin and the older man's mockery was not calculated to improve it.

"Do I ask you about growing coffee?"

"No. But I'd be happy to tell you if you did."

"This is police business."

"What? Snake-bite?"

"Yes."

"Look, Curtis —" He was serious now. His pale eyes were shrewd and penetrating. "One of the things you learn in a job like mine is to keep your mouth shut and your eyes open. If you say so, I'll do just that. I'm not a policeman. I don't belong to the Administration. You can blow this island off the map and I'll still have a job. On the other hand, I may be able to help you."

"How?"

"There's trouble blowing up. I have no more than an inkling of what it may be — but one thing I'm sure of, this Lansing business is part of it."

"How do you know that?"

The question was sharp with professional interest. Nelson shrugged.

"I don't *know* anything. I'm guessing. I'm guessing that you're taking Sonderfeld with you for a reason. I'm guessing that you're not satisfied with the report from the village and that you're going to make inquiries on your own account. I'm suggesting — only suggesting, mind you — that if you give me a little of the background I may be able to pick up some information while you're away. I presume I'll dine at the house. Wee Georgie's a gossipy sort of soul. Mrs. Sonderfeld will probably react to a little sympathy. And sometimes the onlooker sees more of the game than the man on the field."

Curtis nodded slowly.

"That's fair enough. But why? What's your interest?"

Nelson chuckled and gave a comical shrug of defeat.

"Damned if I know. I'm breaking the habit of a lifetime. Perhaps I like you. Perhaps I don't like Sonderfeld. "Perhaps..." His eyes darkened. "Perhaps I'm scared of a place where a man can be killed in his cups and never know what struck him. Perhaps I need an ally as much as you do. Anyway, there it is. Take it or leave it."

Seconds passed while Lee Curtis stood, silent and abstracted, staring out across the valley. Then his tight features relaxed into a boyish grin. He held out his hand.

"All right. I'll take it! Walk with me down to the Kiap house. I'll talk to you as we go."

As he walked slowly across the plantation and up the gravelled path that led to the bungalow, Kurt Sonderfeld took stock of his situation. The first glance showed him a neat profit. His dominion over the sorcerer was established. The swift and sudden death of Lansing proved that. With Lansing gone, one major danger to his project was removed. His mouth was stopped, such evidence as he might have given was stifled for ever. Unless...

A new fear halted him in his tracks – Lansing's notes.

The man was a scholar, a meticulous recorder. Was there any mention of Sonderfeld's activities in the notebooks which Curtis was bound to find when he came to collect the belongings of the dead man? He weighed the possibility, measured the risk. Then he was no longer afraid. There might be nothing. At most, there would be the scrawled and cryptic jottings, the groundwork of a thesis that would never be written. They would harm him no more and probably a good deal less than Lansing's blunt challenge over the whisky.

He became aware that Wee Georgie was standing beside him, studying him with shrewd and furtive eyes. He turned abruptly and began giving him orders for the conduct of the plantation during his absence. Wee Georgie listened and nodded continuously like a mandarin figure. He knew it all by heart. He knew exactly how little he could do and still escape the wrath of his master. Then, without warning, Sonderfeld heeled to a new tack.

"Then, there is the girl."

"N'Daria, boss?"

"That's right."

Wee Georgie leered happily.

"I'll keep me eye on her, boss. Never fear. I'll see she doesn't go whorin' around with the –"

"Shut up!" said Sonderfeld harshly. "Shut up and listen to me."

"Yes, boss." Wee Georgie was fervently contrite.

"You will have nothing to do with the girl, nothing to say to her. Let her go where she wants, do what she will. But you will arrange that her every movement is watched by your women or by one of the work-boys. When I come back, I shall want a complete account, hour by hour, day and night. Understand?"

"Yes, boss. Yes ... leave it to me. Those girls of mine have got eyes in their backsides."

"Keep your own eyes open, Georgie – and your ears, too. Don't drink too much. There are things moving that you do not understand. I will not have them complicated by a babbling fool with a bellyful of liquor."

"You can trust me, boss. You know that."

"I know, Georgie." His thin lips were a smiling threat. "I know that I can trust you. Why else would I have kept you alive so long."

With that, he left him, a flabby, quaking wreck, cold in the warm sunshine. Wee Georgie shivered and licked his dry lips. He thought he had never needed a drink so badly.

As Sonderfeld came closer to the bungalow, he realized with something of a shock that he did not know what to say to his wife. In a curious fashion, he was, for the first time, afraid of her. When, in the past, he had meditated the death of Lansing it had been part of his pleasure to anticipate her reaction when he told her, bluntly and brutally, that her lover was dead. He had framed little speeches of mockery, little tricks of surprise to recall the presence of her lover, even when she was prepared to forget him.

Now, with Curtis alert and Nelson a shrewd and prying presence, with his plans for the pig festival so near to fruition, he could not afford the luxury of cruelty. So he must be gentle with her, grave, considerate, even tender, as if regretful of the past and faintly hopeful for the future of their married life. If he could not deceive her, at least he might puzzle her long enough to lull her suspicions of himself.

Then, when Curtis was gone, and Nelson, when the valley was his, and his the dominion of all the mountains, he could abandon himself to the luxury of tormenting her with mockery of her lover's death.

At the foot of the steps he paused to compose his features in an expression of seemly grief. Then he walked into the house.

Gerda was in the living-room arranging a great fan-shaped display of gladioli. She looked up when he entered, and greeted him with the polite indifference that was habitual between them.

"Hullo, Kurt."

Across the polished table he faced her. His eyes were grave, his lips were almost tender.

"I'm afraid I have bad news for you, Gerda."

"Bad news?"

She was only mildly surprised. He hesitated as if at a loss for words. He stumbled a little, stammered over

93

the first awkward phrase. It was a magnificent performance.

"I – You may think I find a pleasure in this. Believe me, I am surprised that I do not. I feel grief for him – and grieve for you. Max Lansing is dead !"

"No !"

Her performance matched his own for depth and subtlety. She hid her face in her hands as if trying to blot out a vision of monstrous horror. Her voice came to him in a muffled whisper.

"How? When did he die?"

"He was drunk last night. He was bitten by a snake and died in his sleep. At least that is the report we have had from the luluai. Curtis and I are going up to – to make an inspection and bury the poor fellow."

"You are going up?"

Her surprise was genuine now. This was a move she had not expected. Sonderfeld nodded.

"Yes. Curtis wants a death certificate, possibly a post-mortem. Don't ask me why. I don't know. In any case, I am hardly in a position to refuse."

"When are you going?"

"As soon as I have changed my clothes and packed some instruments."

"I'll help you."

"There is no need."

"I should like to do it. You have been kind to me in this – kinder than I could have believed possible with you. I am grateful, Kurt. Please let me help."

Amused by her humble gratitude, elated by the success of his acting, he made no further protest, but went with her to the bedroom. He stripped off his shorts and knee stockings and the white, short-sleeved shirt, and put on a pair of denim slacks, greenhide jungle boots, webbing gaiters, and a long-sleeved shirt of military pattern. It would be a long walk and the insects would be bad; it was wise to leave as little as possible of the body exposed.

94

While he was dressing, Gerda packed shaving gear and a box of cigars and a clean change in his canvas shoulder bag, and laid out the small leather case of surgical instruments. She gathered up his discarded clothes and laid them in a heap on the bed for the house-boy to collect. She rubbed his hands and his face with repellent oil and went down on her knees to adjust the straps of his gaiters. Nothing more was said between them, but Sonderfeld watched her with cynical amusement, remembering the first days of her servitude to him.

He was so absorbed in this refinement of pleasure that he quite forgot the bamboo tube which he always carried in the pocket of his white shorts.

He was half-way over the mountains with Lee Curtis before he remembered it.

Long before it had reached Patrol Officer Lee Curtis the news of Lansing's death was reported to Père Louis. His village was only a few miles from Lansing's, and the commerce between them was easy and constant. A man with a load of canes met an old woman leading a blind pig. They whispered a moment, furtively, fearfully, and then they parted.

The woman met a man and his son armed with bows and arrows out on the hunt for Bird of Paradise plumes. She hailed them and they came to her with reluctance, but when they had heard her low-spoken message, they turned back, running in the direction of the village.

The man and his son passed the taro patch where his wife was working. They told her the news in hurried undertones, then went back to the hunt. The woman told another woman and she told her husband's father.

The old man told the luluai and the luluai who was a Christian told the catechist, and so, like a coin passed from hand to hand, the news came finally to the old priest.

The white man who lived in the next village was dead

of the snake-sorcery and the man who had killed him was Kumo, the cassowary man.

Père Louis sat for a long time in the cool darkness of his hut, weighing the whispered words of the catechist. The burden of his years lay heavy on his shoulders and the accumulated guilt of other men was an oppression to his tired spirit.

Death held no terrors for him, but he shared the terror of those who met it unprepared, without shriving or viaticum. To Lansing it had come in the days of his adultery, at a moment when he was farthest from the grace of repentance. It had come violently, as a vengeance, not gently, as a merciful release.

Père Louis bowed his face in his hands and prayed the last loving prayer of the Crucified.

"Father, forgive them, for they know not what they do."

Lansing was a lost and lonely man, but not an evil one. The evil was in those who had compassed his death and set him beyond the reach of mercy, when mercy was his greatest need.

There was Sonderfeld, cold, calculating, saturnine, a newcomer from the monstrous twilight of Europe. There was Kumo, the man from the old time, before the Decalogue, before the New Promise – Kumo who had been offered salvation but had rejected it, turning back to the groves of Baal and Dagon and the god who was a great pig. Between these two there was a bond, a dark brotherhood whose beginning was pride and whose end was death and eternal damnation.

The old priest asked himself what he should do. The dead were beyond his help. His business was with the living. Sonderfeld and Kumo were out of his reach – if not yet beyond the reach of God Almighty. Curtis was a man bound by an oath of service to a cause that was not his own. There remained Gerda, the woman with the warm body and the cold heart, and N'Daria, the brown girl who had followed the drums and the flutes and was now lost in the wilderness of sin.

So the light came to him, clear and unmistakable. Let the dead bury their dead. Let Curtis and his police-boys do what must be done for Lansing. He himself would go back to the bungalow.

He had his catechist beat the drum that called his Christians to prayer, and when they came huddling into the small chapel he put on the black stole and the black chasuble and offered the Mass for the Dead. After the Communion he spoke to them, exhorting them to persevere in faith and prayer and to arm themselves with innocence against the powers of evil. Then he gave them the last blessing and the ritual dismissal and heard their voices raised with his in the invocation to Saint Michael, Prince of the Heavenly Spirits, for defence against Satan and the pillagers of souls.

When the last of his little congregation had filed out of the chapel, he took off his vestments and knelt a few moments in prayer before the altar.

Then he stood up, walked out into the bright sunshine, and took the road to Sonderfeld's plantation.

CHAPTER 8

"FINISHED yet?"

Curtis looked up from his reading of Lansing's note-books to ask the question of Sonderfeld, who was still bending over the body, intent on the grim business of evisceration and dismemberment.

"Very soon now."

Sonderfeld's voice was cool and professional.

It was morning. They were in Lansing's hut, Curtis slightly in shadow at the table, Sonderfeld in the shaft of light from the doorway working under the curious

97

stares of the villagers who were held back by the line of police-boys standing with rifles at the porte, motionless as ebony statues.

They had come to the village late the previous night. They had made a cursory inspection of the scene, then posted a guard of police and retired to spend the night in the Kiap house. When morning came, Curtis had called the villagers together and questioned the luluai in their presence without shaking his story in the slightest particular. All the evidence confirmed its truth : the position of the body, the scars of the snake-bite, the liquor, and the shattered glass. No jury would have disputed a verdict of death by misadventure.

But Curtis was still not satisfied. He made a thorough search of the hut, collected all Lansing's belongings, listed them carefully, and had the police-boys parcel them in woven mats for transport back to the bungalow and later to Goroka. The note-books he had kept apart to read while Sonderfeld did his post-mortem.

The body was already puffy with poison and incipient decay. The ants had begun to crawl on it and the big bush rats had begun to gnaw at the extremities, but Sonderfeld went about his work with calm and precision. His strong hands were encased in rubber gloves and a sweating police-boy stood near him with a wooden bowl of steaming water, a clean towel, and a cake of disinfectant soap.

When he had finished, he straightened up, stripped off the gloves, washed his hands carefuly and gave directions in pidgin for the sterilizing of his gloves and instruments. Then he turned to Curtis.

"It is done."

"What's the verdict?"

Sonderfeld shrugged.

"As before. He must have been very drunk. His stomach was still full of unabsorbed spirit."

"The cause of death?"

"Paralysis of the motor centres, following the snake-bite. One hour, two perhaps, after he had been bitten."

"Can you identify the poison?"

"No. I have not the knowledge for that. I doubt if anyone has yet."

Curtis closed the book with a snap and stood up. He pointed to the desk and the vacant chair.

"Mind writing me a report on it? Might as well get everything straight now."

Sonderfeld made a gesture of indifference, sat down at the rough table, and wrote his report with Lansing's pencil on Lansing's note-paper. His hand was steady, his script was firm and business-like. When he had finished, he scribbled a signature, folded the paper, and handed it to Curtis, who slipped it into his note-book and buttoned it in his breast-pocket.

"What now?"

"We bury him," said Curtis simply. "We bury him and then go home."

They buried him under the shade of the tangket-trees on the outer fringe of the village. They buried him deep to keep him safe from the snuffling pigs, and Curtis recited the Lord's Prayer while Sonderfeld stood bare-headed and the villagers waited in theatrical grief and the police-boys stood rigidly at attention. Then they fired a salute over the open grave, Curtis threw in the first handful of black earth and the natives filled the hole with their hands, chattering and laughing and stamping the earth down with their bare feet.

They marked the grave with a big square stone and left him there – lonely in death as he had been in life – loveless, barren of achievement, Max Lansing, crowned with dust, naked in the naked earth of the oldest island on the planet.

At the moment of Max Lansing's burial in the mountain village, Gerda Sonderfeld, Theodore Nelson, and Père Louis sat together on the stoop of the bungalow.

Between them on the table lay the small tube of

bamboo which N'Daria had given to Sonderfeld. Père Louis leant forward and lifted the tube between the thumb and forefinger of his right hand. Gerda and Nelson watched him, fascinated. His eyes were hard, his mouth was grim under the grey beard.

"Tell me –" He gestured with the shiny, brown tube. "Tell again how you came by this."

"I picked it up in the bedroom," said Gerda. "It fell from the pocket of Kurt's trousers when the house-boy came to take them to the wash."

"Do you know what it is?" asked Theodore Nelson.

"I do."

"Have you seen it before?" It was Gerda's question this time.

"I have seen others like it," said Père Louis gravely. He slipped the cap from the tube and showed them the noisome, clotted wad inside. "In the other cases there was a handful of moss, a fragment of bark cloth. But the meaning is the same."

He replaced the cap and laid the tube on the table.

"What is the meaning, Father?" Gerda's anxious eyes searched his face.

"Before I tell you that, madame, I should like to know," – he turned his grim old eyes on Theodore Nelson – "what is your part in this?"

It was Gerda who answered for him, eagerly as for a trusted ally.

"Mr. Nelson has been asked by the Patrol Officer to look after me and to pick up whatever information he can during the absence of proper authority."

The answer seemed to satisfy the little priest. He nodded absently and spent a long time examining the wrinkled, mottled skin on the backs of his small hands. Then he spoke, slowly and carefully, like a man whose strength is running out, and for whom even the effort of speech is a costly loss.

"What you saw in that tube was the life of a human being. The cottonwool is impregnated with the spittle

100

and the blood – and I believe – the seed of a living man. Whoever holds this tube, holds that man in bondage, because he holds his life and can compass his death."

"My husband!" The words were a long-drawn whisper of horror.

Père Louis nodded soberly.

"It would seem so."

"But – but –" Nelson stammered the words in his excitement. "To whom does that belong – that messy thing?"

Père Louis turned his grave, tired eyes on Gerda.

"Can you answer that, madame?"

Without hesitation she rose to the challenge.

"I believe so. I think it belongs to Kumo the Sorcerer. I think also that he is the man through whom my husband killed Max Lansing."

"God Almighty!"

Theodore Nelson swore softly and mopped his clammy forehead. Père Louis was staring down at his old and knotted hands. It was a long time before any of them spoke again. Nelson was the first to break the silence.

"Does – does this thing really work?"

Père Louis nodded sombrely.

"It works, my friend; be in no doubt of that. It works, as fear and superstition always work to corruption and death and the destruction of man's immortal soul."

"How in God's name would he get such a thing?"

Père Louis spread his hands, palm upwards, on the table as if to emphasize the simplicity of the answer.

"He would get it through a woman, a woman whom he would send to seduce this man and fornicate with him. It is as blunt and as easy as that."

Nelson shot a sidelong glance at Gerda, then averted his eyes in shame and embarrassment. Père Louis began to light his pipe, puffing furiously and sending great clouds of foul smoke curling over the table. Gerda alone was calm and contained. She said flatly, "The woman, of course, is N'Daria. She works for my husband. She is passionately in love with him. She would do anything he asked."

Père Louis nodded agreement, but said nothing. It was left to Theodore Nelson to lay down the final pieces in the pattern.

"So that's what Lansing meant about the cargo cult and the domination of the tribes. That's why he was killed, because he came too close to the truth. That's why –"

"That is why we must say nothing of this until I have had the chance to speak to Curtis and decide what we must do." The old priest picked up the bamboo tube and put it in his pocket. He pushed aside his chair and stood up. "Now, my friend, if you will excuse us, I should like a word in private with madame. I suggest you walk in the garden awhile. The fresh air will do you good."

Still dabbing at his damp forehead, Theodore Nelson made an awkward stumbling exit, and Gerda was left alone with Père Louis.

The old priest laid his hand on hers with a gentle, comforting gesture.

"Now, my child, we will talk of things that concern only the two of us. But first –" His lined face relaxed into a boyish grin. "But first I should like a drink – a strong one!"

She brought him whisky and a jug of iced water. She waited patiently while he sank the first drink at a gulp and sipped at the second with careful relish. His silence and his deliberation troubled her not at all. Of all the people who surrounded her in this time of shame and crisis Père Louis was the one she trusted most. There was in his stringy old body an enduring strength. His spirit was endowed with a patient, compassionate wisdom to which the others were strangers. He had the bluntless of the man who has faced the final consequences of his belief, the tenderness of the man who knows the burden that belief lays on the shoulders of weak men and women. His presence rested her, gave her time and courage to collect her scattered strength.

Père Louis finished his drink and set down the empty glass.

"Now," he said gently, "we will talk about you."

"About me, Father?" she took it calmly enough, but she was wary as a cat.

"About you and your immortal soul."

She smiled bitterly.

"You are the first man I have met who was interested in my soul."

Père Louis did not smile. His eyes were grave and gentle.

"Max Lansing? Did you love him?"

"No."

"Do you love your husband?"

"I hate him."

"So ... you are married to a man you hate. You have committed adultery with a man you do not love."

"With many men, Father."

"Did it make you happy, my child?"

She shrugged, still smiling the rueful, crooked smile.

"Long ago, Father, I learnt that I should not expect happiness. I have tried to make myself content with what is left to me."

"Do you believe in God, child?"

"No."

"And yet you are a Pole. You were born and baptized in the Church."

"Yes."

"What happened to you? What happened to you that you came to lose the one thing that might have made you happy?"

There was no reproach in the old voice, only an attentive earnestness as if he were a doctor probing a deep and painful wound. She felt no resentment – she was content to follow the line of his questioning, answering simply and without evasion because she had nothing to hide.

"There was a time, Father, when I needed God and He was not there. There was a time when I called on Him and He did not answer. It is as simple as that."

"Tell me about it."

She told him. She told him of the war and of the rape of the eastern cities. She told him of the long horror that ended with her meeting with Reinach and the new horror that had grown out of the same meeting. She told him of her maiming and her servitude. She told him how Reinach became Sonderfeld and of the monstrous bargain she had made with him. She told of their life together and of their loves apart; and, when she had finished, it was as if a weight had been lifted from her shoulders and a tight hand had loosened its grip around her heart. Père Louis lowered his eyes to hide the pity and the tenderness and the old, foolish tears. He took her white, slack hand between his own rough palms and patted it gently.

"To say that I am sorry for you, child, is to say an empty and a barren thing. I am a priest, an unworthy shepherd of the flock of Christ. You belong to that flock and you belong to me, though you have wandered a long, hard way from the fold. I say to you now, you do not need pity. You need strength and love and the grace to forgive others as God is ready to forgive you."

She made a little shrugging gesture of despair.

"I have strength, I think. Otherwise I should not have endured so much and so long. But love...? Perhaps I am incapable of love, as I am incapable of bearing children?"

"No!" Père Louis' voice was suddenly strong in rejection. "You think you are incapable of love, because all these years you have made the act of love an act of self-torment, an act of revenge upon the man who has wronged you. To sin with love and passion is one thing. It is a sin according to nature, but a sin that carries the seed of its own salvation. To sin without love is a perversion, a monstrous contradiction that will debase you

104

lower than the man you wish to hurt. Child. . . ." The old man's voice was warm again and soft with compassion. "Child, I am an old man. Like Solomon with all his years upon him, I have seen evil under the sun. But I have seen good, too – much good – so much that I am daily humbled and grateful to the good God. Believe me, I do not sell you cheap words. I am no huckster of the Gospel. I am a tired, spent man; I have no traffic but with the truth. Bend to me, child, bend a little and see at your feet the love of God, bright and beautiful, like the flowers in your garden."

Gerda Sonderfeld buried her face in her hands and wept. The old man stood beside her and patted her dark hair like a father comforting a grieving child. Then, when all her tears were spent and she lifted her ravaged face, he fished in his pocket for a handkerchief and handed it to her with a wry grin.

"There now, already it begins to be better. Dry your eyes and we will see what can be done to mend this madness in the valleys."

Père Louis was in a double dilemma.

Possession of the bamboo tube set him in a position of some power against both Sonderfeld and Kumo. Yet his status as a missionary deprived him of the authority to use it. There was only one authority in the valley – Cadet Patrol Officer Lee Curtis. He, being young and unsure of himself, might well resent the intrusion of the Church into secular affairs. He might, with more reason, object to paying the penalty for the Church's mistakes – and mistakes were very possible when one was dealing with the abnormal psychologies of paranoic modern and primitive man.

Père Louis found himself wishing, as he had wished many times in the last days, that George Oliver were on patrol again and not beating his head and bruising his heart against mountains of paper in the District Commissioner's office at Goroka.

George Oliver would have understood and approved what he wanted to do. He had made his reputation by gambles such as this one. But George Oliver was two days away behind the southern barrier.

There was another problem, too – a moral one. Gerda Sonderfeld hated her husband and was prepared to revenge herself upon him for the death of her lover. To invite her co-operation in Sonderfeld's downfall would be to lay on her and on himself a new burden of guilt. He was, first and foremost, a priest, and sin was to him a disorder worse than final chaos. Whatever he did, therefore, he must do without her knowledge.

He needed time, prayer, and a little solitude, to extricate himself from his dilemma. So, in spite of Gerda's curiosity and disappointment, he took himself off in the direction of the big clump of bamboos that screened the boy-houses from the main bungalow and Gerda's garden.

There, sitting on a mossy log, he made a short prayer and smoked a long, soothing pipe, before he made up his mind what to do.

First, he hailed one of the house-boys and traded him a plug of tobacco for a bamboo container similar in size and texture to Sonderfeld's. He had the boy bring him a wad of cottonwool and, with the aid of spittle, tobacco juice and blood, pricked from his finger, he made a reasonable facsimile of the contents of Sonderfeld's tube.

Then he took the wad containing Kumo's vital juices and transferred it to his own container. In its place he put the tampon he himself had made, closed both tubes and held them side by side in his outstretched hand – the real and the false – while he pondered how he should use them.

The forgery he would return to Gerda, so that Sonderfield would find it when he came home. The original he would keep against the time of final conflict.

He saw it clearly and in detail; the assembly of the tribes in the Lahgi Valley, the tossing plumes, the spilt blood, the bodies of the sacrificial pigs piled high outside the spirit houses. He saw Sonderfeld proclaimed by Kumo as the incarnation of the Red Spirit. He saw himself, small and alone, in the centre of the compound, challenging Sonderfeld for a liar and Kumo for a dupe and holding up his own bamboo capsule in proof of the challenge. He saw the doubt and the uncertainty in Kumo's eyes – for even the great sorcerer could not pierce the bamboo walls to know which man was a liar and which held his life in the hollow of his hand.

The next moment he could not foresee, because this would be the moment of the final gamble, the moment when the shrewd primitive would weigh him against Sonderfeld for truth and credit and strength. This would be the moment in which he would have great need of the sheltering mercy of God, for if he were found wanting, he would be cut down by the stone axes and his blood would be spilt with the spilt blood of the pigs.

He shivered in spite of the warmth, thrust the tube into his pocket and, carrying the other in his clenched fist, walked slowly back to the bungalow.

In the rich darkness of the cool mountain night, Kurt Sonderfeld came home to his bungalow. His bones were weary from the long trek over the mountains, his body stank with fatigue, and his stained clothes were stiff with mud and drying sweat. He was ill-tempered and troubled by the stiff reserve of Lee Curtis, who, in spite of his youth and inexperience, had conducted the investigation with punctilious caution. In spite of the fact that he had found nothing suspicious or at variance with the village story, he was reserved and wary and he made no secret of his displeasure at Sonderfeld's constant questioning.

When, at the first homeward halt, he had asked to see Lansing's manuscript, Curtis had handed it to him without demur. But, as he skimmed it, thumbing quickly through the close-written pages with their cryptic notes in professional jargon, he was conscious that Curtis was watching him closely, studying his face for any reaction of surprise or displeasure. The boy mistrusted him, but Sonderfeld was unable to put a finger on the cause of his distrust. So far as he could see in the first quick glance, there was nothing at all in the notes that could be construed as an accusation. Finally, he shrugged off his fear, but the ill-temper stayed with him the rest of the way home.

More than all, however, the loss of the bamboo tube fretted him. So much depended on his possession of that small, sinister capsule; so much more depended on keeping his possession a secret. If Gerda found it, all would be well. She was indifferent to such things, accustomed to his having about him such trifles of native workmanship.

It was the house-boys who troubled him. If one of them had picked it up, he would be certain to open it – the Highland native is curious as a jackdaw. Then, when he saw what it contained, he would either fall into a gibbering panic or he would keep it for a trade with Kumo or another sorcerer. Either event could spell disaster for Sonderfield.

But, when he came into the bedroom where Gerda was sleeping soundly, he saw on the bedside table a pile of freshly washed handkerchiefs and, on top of them, the bamboo tube. Gerda had found it then. She had done as wives do with a mislaid cuff-link or a forgotten wrist-watch – laid it where he would be sure to see it when he came home.

Sonderfield smiled with satisfaction. His ill-humour fell away from him like a sloughed skin. He thrust the tube into his trouser pocket, then, remembering the mishap of the previous day, thought better of it and put it far back in the drawer of his cabinet and covered it with the handkerchiefs. It would be safe there until he needed it.

He stripped off his soiled clothes, threw a towel over

his arm and walked down to the shower-room to refresh himself for sleep. As he passed the half-open door of the guest-room, he heard the sound of deep, regular breathing, punctuated by an occasional snore. He stopped, pushed the door open and peered into the room. Père Louis was sleeping the sleep of the just and godly. Sonderfeld withdrew frowning.

The presence of the priest puzzled him. He remembered their last meeting and the old man's refusal to visit him again unless he were summoned. He wondered if Gerda had sent for him. Then he remembered that Père Louis' village was close to Lansing's. He would have heard the news before any of them. But why had he come here instead of making straight for Lansing's place?

He chewed on the proposition as he bathed and towelled himself; and, finally, because he could not brook any thought that challenged the perfection of his own planning, he decided that the priest had come to offer sympathy to the friends of the dead man – a natural enough gesture in the isolation of the mountains, where any excuse is good enough for a gathering. Perhaps, too, the old man wanted to make friends again. He would miss the whisky and the regular dinner among civilized people.

Sonderfeld smiled with sour triumph and walked back to the bedroom. He told himself he was a fool to trouble over trifles. Let them suspect what they would; let them hate him as much as they dared; they could not shake a single stone of the empire of Kurt Sonderfeld.

He threw himself on the bed, drew the covers about his shoulders, and lapsed immediately into a dreamless sleep.

He did not hear the running feet of the cassowary bird pounding down the mountain, drumming past the village, thundering up the slope, towards the laboratory where N'Daria tossed uneasily in her lonely bed.

Père Louis heard them and sat bolt upright, instantly

awake. The habit of years was strong in him, he had lived through times and in places where death walked the jungle paths; and more than one lonely missionary had fallen under the stone axes and the heavy clubs of the people he had come to save. He knew, too, that the cassowary bird does not stir abroad at night, but sleeps like other birds during the hours of darkness.

The muffled crescendo could have only one meaning. Evil was abroad under the stars. The village slept and the kundus were silent, but the sorcerers were active about their dark business of perversion.

He listened intently. The running feet were closer. They were passing the village. They were turning up the slope towards the plantation. He threw off the covers, dressed himself hurriedly, and crept out of the house.

The night was empty of all but stars and shadowy trees, but the air vibrated with the sound of drumming feet coming closer and closer yet. Père Louis crossed himself and invoked the protection of Christ and His Virgin Mother and walked slowly down the path to meet the oncoming footsteps.

N'Daria heard them, too, and trembled with terror in the darkness. She buried her head under the blankets, but she could not shut out the sound of their inexorable approach. She knew what they meant. Kumo was coming for her as she had known he must come, now that Sonderfeld had rejected her.

She had betrayed her lover and had been betrayed in her turn. Now her lover was coming to exact vengeance, the terrible, dark vengeance that only a sorcerer could exact.

Ever since that night she had lived in constant terror. She had not dared to go to the kunande. She had not set foot in the village. She had hidden herself even from the work-boys and had kept herself in the laboratory hut, trying frantically to concentrate on the tasks that Sonderfeld had set her, but that were now without meaning or potency. She was lost and she knew it. She had tried to live in two worlds, and in both her foothold had crumbled. She had rejected her own people. The white man had rejected her. The knowledge he had given her was no armour against the secret wisdom of the sorcerers.

Fearful, alone, full of guilt and remorse, she could do nothing but lie there, shivering and helpless, while the footbeats came closer and closer, and finally stopped outside the window of the hut.

CHAPTER 9

AT first it was a small, insistent scraping, like the brushing of a windy branch against the windowpane. N'Daria lay rigid under blankets and pretended to be asleep. Then the scraping became a hammering of knuckles, rapid and rhythmic like the beat of a tiny drum. This too, she tried to ignore, but the pulse never slackened and the noise seemed to multiply in the hollow pipes of the bamboo walls until it filled the whole room and vibrated in every nerve of her body.

She could bear it no longer. She threw back the covers and looked up. Kumo was staring at her through the window. His eyes were twin coals; his lips were drawn back in a snarling grin that showed his red-stained teeth; his face was distorted into a monstrous mask by pressure against the glass.

She fought down a scream and tried to turn away her eyes from the terrifying vision, but the eyes of Kumo held her petrified; she stared and stared until it seemed that the horror would stifle her. Kumo gestured to her to open the door. Mechanically, like one in a hypnotic trance, she walked through to the laboratory, unlocked the door and let him in.

The night was still and airless, but the impact of his entry was like the rushing of great wind that robbed her of breath and thrust her back and back, until she felt the hard wood of the bench press into her thighs and her spine arched backward in a last futile effort to escape him. He towered over her, tall and menacing, his painted face hideous, his plumes tossing, the skin of his breast shining with sweat and oil.

If he had touched her, she would have crumpled at his feet. Instead, he stood there, grinning like a tusked beast, his eyes commanding her so that she could not look away, but must stare and stare until his face swelled and swelled like a bladder, blotting out the room, blotting out the stars that shone through the opened doorway, until there was nothing left but the pair of fiery eyes full of gloating accusation. Then, as if from a great distance, she heard his voice.

"This is N'Daria who stole my life to give it to the white man."

She tried to answer him but her throat was full of mossy vapour and no sound came. She tried to struggle but her limbs refused their functions. Her breast and her belly were pressed down as if by a great stone.

"This is N'Daria who thought the magic of the white man was greater than the magic of Kumo. The white man is sleeping, N'Daria. He is weary from his journey over the mountains. He will not come to you until the morning."

She heard him laugh and the sound was an enveloping thunder. His eyes held hers, immovable in the terror of it.

"The white man holds my life, but he cannot touch me while he sleeps. Now we shall make proof of the magic of Kumo. Feel it, N'Daria! There is an arrow in your belly! Feel it!"

He made no movement. He did not touch her even with a finger-tip; but she writhed and twisted in agony, clutching at her middle, her face distorted in a soundless scream.

Kumo watched her, grinning with pleasure. Then,

with the sound of his voice the pain left her and she was still again, stiff and motionless as a cataleptic. His fiery eyes were a mockery, his voice was a bubbling chuckle.

"There is more, N'Daria. There is more. Your mouth is full of thorns and your throat is choked with pebbles. Feel them!"

Her eyes bulged, her cheeks puffed out. The arteries of her throat swelled and her diaphragm was sucked in under the rib-cage. She was in the final agony of suffocation before he released her again, and watched her retching with relief, her face grey and streaming with sweat.

So, in the timeless seconds of the hypnotic syncope, he led her through one agony after another. He made her flesh crawl with stinging bull-ants. He set a fire in her brain and a gnawing animal in her stomach. He made her joints crack as if distended on a rack. He made her feel the lash of canes and the mutilation of stone knives. And still he did not touch her.

The whole performance lasted only a few minutes, but before he released her she had run the gamut of torment, endured a lifetime of affliction. Then she stood before him, trembling and broken, the tears streaming down her cheeks, her mouth slobbering open, her nerves twitching uncontrollably.

Kumo licked his lips, savouring the salt tang of vengeance. Then he took from his arm-band the same bamboo capsule with which he had killed Max Lansing.

N'Daria gasped with the impact of this final terror, but she had no strength to withdraw from it.

"You know what this is, N'Daria?"

"Yes." It was a stifled whisper.

"You took my life, N'Daria. You took my life and gave it to the white man. Now I shall take yours and give it to the spotted snake, and the white man will never know."

She could not move. She could not cry out. She could only stand and wait as he brought the tube closer and closer to her body so that when the snake was released, it would erupt like a spring and fasten on the tight skin of her breast. Wide-eyed, she saw Kumo's fingers tighten on the cap. She smelt the foulness of his breath and felt his trembling eagerness in this moment of triumph.

Then, sharp and sudden as a cracking stick, came the voice of Père Louis.

"Drop it, Kumo. Drop it !"

The bamboo capsule fell, bounced once, and rolled into the shadows against the wall. N'Daria crumpled to the floor in a dead faint. Kumo and the priest faced each other.

The sorcerer towered over the old man like a grotesque, carven idol, his painted face was twisted with fury and in his eyes was the naked evil of all the centuries. Père Louis' blood ran like ice in his veins, his old flesh crawled with horror. This was Satan made manifest. This was the true biblical phenomenon of diabolic possession, in the presence of which even prayer was stifled and faith rocked for one perilous moment on the razor-edge of despair.

But only for a moment.

Père Louis' hand closer over the rosary in his pocket. With a sharp commanding gesture he thrust the small wooden crucifix full in the face of the sorcerer. His voice was sharp as a sword blade in the old and terrible command :

"*Retro me Sathanas!* Get thee behind me, Satan !"

Kumo's body was wrenched with a sudden convulsive tremor. He yelped like an animal and a small yellow foam spilled from the corners of his mouth. Then he turned and ran from the hut, and Père Louis stood rocking on his feet and listening to the thudding flight of the cassowary man under the dark drooping of the tangket-trees.

Down in the Kiap house, Lee Curtis woke with a start to find Père Louis bending over him.

"Get up. Dress yourself. Light the lamp. I want to talk to you."

"What the devil!" Curtis rubbed his eyes and tried to orient himself. By rights the old priest should have been in his village, miles away. His presence on the plantation was the final straw in the day's burden of irritations and mysteries. "What's the trouble? What are you doing here?"

"Keep your voice down. Do as I say. I will talk to you when you are awake."

Stumbling and cursing softly, Lee Curtis dressed himself and lit the lamp, while Nelson, awakened by their voices, sat bolt upright on his bed-roll and fumbled for his spectacles. Then, when they were settled in the small circle of light, Curtis said bluntly, "All right, Father, let's have it."

"First," said Père Louis, "I want to show you how Lansing was killed."

He held the bamboo tube up for their inspection.

"God Almighty!" stuttered Nelson. "Not another one."

Curtis leant forward to take the tube from his hand, but Père Louis drew it back sharply.

"Careful. This one is dangerous. Look!"

He tilted it under the lamp so that they could see the small circle of air-holes punched in the pithy cap.

"Now listen."

He shook the tube and held it first to Curtis's ear, then to Nelson's. They heard a tiny movement and friction against the walls of the barrel.

"What's that?" It was Nelson who put the question. Curtis was tight-lipped and thoughtful.

"Snake-sorcery," said Père Louis simply. "Inside that tube is a small and deadly snake. The sorcerers catch them and imprison them in these tubes, sometimes with a fragment of the clothing of those they wish to murder. They irritate the snake with noise and movement and hunger, so that when it is released it will attack the first object on which it alights."

"Where did you get it?" Lee Curtis's voice was grim.

"From Kumo. Not ten minutes ago he tried to murder N'Daria in the laboratory up there. Fortunately, I had heard him coming and was ready for him."

"He – he gave it to you?" Nelson was stammering with excitement and fear.

"Not exactly. I – I commanded him in the name of God. He fled from me and left the tube behind."

"Just like that," said Curtis softly.

"As you say, just like that."

"And the girl?"

"I left her in the hut. She is badly frightened, but unharmed. But you see" – Père Louis leant forward and gestured emphatically – "we now have the picture complete. Nelson will have told you that Sonderfeld has in his possession the life-juices of Kumo."

Curtis nodded.

"Through Kumo he murdered Lansing."

"And tried to murder the girl."

The old priest shook his head.

"No, that was a private matter – vengeance against the woman who had betrayed him. The rest is clear. Through Kumo, Sonderfeld can dominate the tribes. I am guessing at this, but I think that Sonderfeld will use the pig festival to have himself proclaimed by Kumo as the incarnation of the Red Spirit."

"Lansing thought the same thing. That's why he was killed."

"Of course."

Nelson burst in excitedly. "Then you've got all you want. Arrest Sonderfeld. Arrest Kumo. You've broken the trouble before it starts."

Curtis shook his head.

"It won't work, Nelson."

"Why not, for God's sake?"

"Evidence. I've got no evidence against Sonderfeld. I've got nothing against Kumo except attempted murder.

and to make that one stick I've got to tip my hand to Sonderfeld."

"But you just can't sit here and –"

"Look, Nelson!" The boyish face was tired and lined with anxiety. "Look! When you're up here, you feel as though you're ten thousand years behind the times. You are, too, in a way. But just fifty miles over those hills is Goroka: civilization, the law, the twentieth century – and the United Nations. They've got a long reach; and whatever I think myself, whatever I'd like to do, I'm still amenable to them. Sonderfeld's the man I want. I can't get him until I stand him in a dock and produce evidence that a judge and jury will accept. At this moment I've got nothing – nothing at all."

"You've got Kumo."

"I want Sonderfeld."

Père Louis wagged his beard like a wise old goat and said gravely. "Curtis is right. Destroy Sonderfeld and there will be no more trouble in the valleys. But you cannot destroy him without evidence – and, I tell you, you will get no more than you have now."

"There's the girl. If she would talk . . .?"

"After what she has endured tonight, she will not talk. I tell you that now. You could take her a hundred miles from here and she would not talk because she would still live in dread of the sorcerers."

"Time!" said Curtis suddenly. "Time is the problem. Whatever we do must be done before the pig festival. If not, we're going to have the biggest blow-up for twenty years – punitive expeditions, the lot! Time, time, time!"

He beat his fist angrily into his palm in frustration and puzzlement.

"When is the pig festival?" asked Nelson.

"That's the trouble. We don't know. It's not a matter of dates, you see. The tribes are moving into the Lahgi Valley, the outer ones first, then the nearer. These folk down here could move tomorrow or the next day. Once they're all assembled, the elders and the sorcerers

117

set the day for the big show – the rest is all preparation and build-up. After what's happened, I think Kumo and Sonderfeld will see that the big ceremony starts almost immediately. That's my problem, don't you see? I can't leave the place. I'd like to discuss it with my people at Goroka, but I can't."

"If I might make a suggestion?" said Père Louis mildly.

"Go ahead, Father. We're in a jam. I'll listen to anything that will help us out of it."

"Good!" The old man's voice was eager and sharp with authority. "This is what you will do. You will write a report now. I will help you do it to save time. Then you will send your best and most reliable runner over the mountains to Goroka. You will send him before dawn so that Sonderfeld will not know. It will take him – how long?"

"A day and a half – say forty hours. It's a long haul even for a good man."

"Very well. Who will deal with the matter at Goroka?"

"Oliver, I should think, George Oliver. He's the A.D.O. in charge of this territory. He was the man who opened it up."

"So! While you are waiting for Oliver, you will go about your duties in the normal fashion. You, Nelson, will concern yourself with the plantation and with nothing else. I shall return to my village and I shall say nothing about what has happened tonight. The girl will say nothing either. I have seen to that. Nothing will happen till the pig festival."

Curtis frowned in dissatisfaction.

"But that's the whole point. It's two days down and two days up – four days at the very best. What happens if Oliver doesn't get here in time?"

It was a long moment before Père Louis answered.

"Then, my friend, you will take your police-boys and go up to the Lahgi Valley. To get there, you will have to pass through my village. I shall be waiting and I shall go up with you."

"And then?"

"Then," said Père Louis with a wry grin, "we shall trust in the power of God and a small stratagem of my own. I confess I am not happy about using it, but at the worst, I shall do so."

"Do you mind telling me what it is?"

"I should prefer not to tell you . . . yet. But if your senior officer arrives in time, I shall tell him."

Curtis was irritated by this apparent reflection on his capacity. He challenged the little priest.

"Why tell Oliver and not me?"

"Because, my son," said Père Louis soberly, "you are a young man who is bearing with some courage a big responsibility. I do not wish to add to that responsibility the burden of a grave decision."

"What sort of decision?"

"The life or death of a man."

"But you'd let Oliver make it?" He was still fidgeting under the slight.

"Oh, yes," said Père Louis, simply, "I would let Oliver make it. I know him, you see – he knows me. And both of us know the tribes. Now I suggest we write this report and send your messenger on his way."

Forty minutes later a fuzzy-headed police-boy was trotting southward over the switchback trails that led to Goroka. He carried no rifle. His bayonet was strapped between his shoulders and in his shining bandolier he carried the reports of Lee Curtis and Père Louis on the situation in the high valleys. His eyes rolled in his head and he licked his lips as he padded up the ridges and down into the black hollows of the defiles. He was a coastal boy from Madang. This country was strange and frightening to him. Its speech was strange to him and he had no talisman against its magic.

He was so scared that he did the fifty miles to Goroka in thirty-three hours.

CHAPTER 10

GEORGE OLIVER was a disappointed man. He was forty-five years of age and he had reached the limit of his stretch – Assistant District Officer, third in the small pyramid of authority whose apex was the District Commissioner and whose base was the thin line of cadet patrol officers strung out over ten thousand square miles of half-controlled territory. He knew it and he knew why, but the knowledge was no salve to his pride.

More than twenty years of his life had been spent in the Territory and his record of service was unblemished. He had come as a cadet when the Highlands were a blank space on a green map; and he himself had opened up and brought under control more territory than any other single man in the service. His work during the Japanese occupation had earned him a D.S.O. and a Military Cross, and his knowledge of the tribes was intimate and encyclopaedic. Yet promotion had passed him by. The higher honours of the service had been denied him. He knew now that they were beyond his reach.

The defect was in himself. He was no diplomat. He lacked the subtlety to sway with the eddies of politics, to profit from the influence of men whose experience and knowledge were less than his own, but who understood the devious shifts of the lobbies and the arts of patronage and preferment. His trenchant decisions were often unpalatable. His raw tongue had made him many enemies. So they left him, close at hand because they needed him, low in the scale of authority because they disliked and often feared him.

Yet, there was much in him to love. He had charm and sympathy, rare justice and a cool courage, and he loved the rich, bursting island and its dark peoples with a deep, passionate attachment, unsoured even by his frustrated ambition. He was generous to his younger colleagues and he covered their mistakes even when he castigated their follies.

Now he sat in his small bare office at Goroka, a lean, compact man, with a tight face and a jutting jaw, and a firm, ironic mouth under the small cavalry moustache. He was a tidy fellow in his person as in his thought. His whites were starched and immaculate. His body, brown as a nut, had an air of disciplined cleanliness. His movements were few and carefully controlled. Absorbed as a student in his texts, he was reading the reports of Père Louis and Lee Curtis on the situation in Sonderfeld's valley.

The runner, sweating and exhausted, had been dismissed to his quarters, glowing with the curt approval of the Kiap, and George Oliver was alone. He was glad of the solitude. He needed it as other men need company, to refresh his spirit and clear his mind of trifles and distractions for concentration on the problem in hand.

The problem was far from simple. Lee Curtis's report, written in haste and anxiety, was not likely to appeal to the District Commissioner, a shrewd, subtle fellow, who liked his files kept dry and academic against the possibility of inquiry from Moresby or Canberra or an unscheduled mission from United Nations. Père Louis' hasty addendum was no improvement. The District Commissioner had small sympathy with the Missions, and tribal magic was to him an anthropological oddity better ignored.

These, however, were minor things beside the problem of Sonderfeld himself. The big German stood well with the Administration. His services were a matter of record. The Administration had approved his tenancy. The Administration would be involved in any charges made against him, and would be less than happy with the flimsy case presented by a half-trained youth and an eccentric French cleric.

Yet George Oliver knew that they were right. He had lived too long and too dangerously to be sceptical about tribal unrest and the fermenting influence of the sorcerers. As to Sonderfeld, there had been adventures before him, and their bids for wealth and power were recorded in more than one bloody page of the history of the Territory.

He laid the reports on his desk, covered them carefully with a blotter, and leant back in his chair, pondering.

First he must see the Commissioner and present the reports with his own summary of the situation. The Commissioner would accept it, because then the responsibilty would be shifted to the shoulders of an unpopular subordinate – and because he knew that George Oliver was the best man to deal with an explosive situation like this one.

Then he would go up himself to the valley. He would take two police-boys and a pair of cargo-carriers. He might take twenty or fifty, but they would serve him no better than two against the massed violence of the assembled tribes. It was his job to forestall violence. He had done it before, he could do it again. It wasn't a question of strength, but of courage and understanding and, above all, timing. His mouth relaxed into an ironic grin. They paid him few compliments; they gave him little thanks; but whenever they landed themselves in a mess – "Let George handle it !" He'd still be handling it when they pensioned him off with an O.B.E. to comfort his declining years. To hell with them ! See the Commissioner and get it over. Get on the move again. There was nothing to hold him here but paper and red tape. He would feel better once he started slogging over the hills – brushing the dust off his heart, sweating the sourness out through the pores of his skin.

He was half-way to the door when he remembered Gerda Sonderfeld. He walked slowly back to his desk, fished in the drawer for a packet of cigarettes, lit one and sat on the edge of the table looking out his window at the trim lawn with its border of bright salvias.

Gerda Sonderfeld! She had dismissed him long ago with tender indifference, but she was still an ache in his heart and a slow fire in his blood. Of all the women he had ever met, this was the one with whom he had come nearest to love – the only one who had left him without clinging and without apparent regret.

It was an old, stale story that had begun during his brief tour of duty on relief in Lae and had ended when Sonderfeld returned from his first survey in the northern valleys. Yet it had touched him more deeply than he was prepared to admit, even to himself. The new Gazette had just been published and his name was not listed among the promotions. He was obsessed with a sense of futility and failure. He was lonelier than he had ever been in his life. He shunned the bar and the club and spent himself, without restraint, in the fierce hunger of a late romance. Gerda had given herself without question and without stint. Her passion charmed him, her rare, perceptive gentleness soothed him. Her uncalculating generosity was a constant surprise. When she dismissed him, his heart was wrenched and he felt empty and old and solitary.

Now he was going back – as her husband's executioner. He toyed with the sardonic thought, but found no pleasure in it. Gerda had made no secret of her cold dislike of her husband; the secret lay in her refusal to leave him for any one of half a dozen men who would gladly have married her – George Oliver among them! He wondered how she would receive him now; how he would bear himself with her. If he indicted Sonderfeld, what then? Would she support her husband in loyalty or would she turn in love to George Oliver, the man who was sending him to criminal trial?

It was a fruitless question, but he worried it like a dog gnawing a dry bone. He told himself he should have more pride, but with the long, disappointing years ahead of him, he knew that pride was a threadbare coat with little warmth in it.

The cigarette burnt down till it scorched his fingers. A long tube of ash fell soundlessly on the desk. He brushed it carefully into the ashtray, stubbed out the butt and walked across the passage to see the District Commissioner.

The District Commissioner had the hard eyes of a politician and the soft voice of a bishop *in partibus infidelium*. He looked like a retired colonel, which he wasn't, and talked like a very canny business man, which he was.

"These reports –" He tapped the stained, scrawled sheets which the runner had brought. "They're no earthly use to me. They say everything and nothing. Curtis expects a revival of the cargo cult in the area under patrol. He believes Sonderfeld is in league with a man named Kumo to set it up. This belief is confirmed by unspecified evidence in the hands of the local missionary, Père – whatever his name is. Curtis expects serious trouble at the pig festival. He suggests we check Sonderfeld's background. What the hell does he mean by that? Sonderfeld was checked and double-checked before he was accepted as a migrant in Australia. If there's anything wrong with his background, that's the business of Immigration, not External Territories."

"Yes, sir," said George Oliver flatly.

There was a pit opening under his feet and one more thrust from the Commissioner would land him at the bottom of it. If Sonderfeld's background was shady, so would Gerda's be. If Sonderfeld were deported from the Territory and Australia, so would Gerda be. And he, George Oliver, would be the instrument of her ruin.

He was relieved when the Commissioner thrust the sketchy report back in his hand with a petulant command.

"Can't put that sort of stuff in the files. You keep 'em

Oliver. Give me say half a page of your own summary for the record – with your suggestions for appropriate action, then we'll deal with it. Yes?"

"No," said George Oliver.

"Oh? Why not?" He spread his palms and set his finger-tips together in a gesture of clerical distaste.

"Because that leaves me holding the can and I'm not paid to do that. You are."

The District Commissioner was nettled, but he knew better than to argue with this sardonic, grinning fellow who knew too many answers for his own good.

"I don't see that you have to be rude about it, Oliver."

"I'm not being rude. I'm stating a fact. I've been in the game too long. I'm tired of being bumped around. Those are the reports. What do you want to do about them?"

"It's your area, isn't it?"

"And yours."

"But you are in direct control. What do you suggest?"

"I'll go up there, take a look, and report when I get back."

"What – er – force will you take?"

"Two police-boys, two cargo-carriers."

The District Commissioner looked relieved. Apparently Oliver didn't expect too much trouble.

"You don't think there's much to worry about then?"

"I didn't say that. Curtis already has his own detachment up there. Between the two of us we should be able to keep things in hand."

"I see. You know the area, of course."

The Commissioner pursed his lips and frowned over the small spire of his finger-tips while he considered the next question. Oliver watched him with ironic amusement. The D.C. was worried. He had reason to be. And George Oliver had no reason to spare him the experience.

"Er – ah – with regard to Sonderfeld. . . ."

"Yes?"

"These reports are a flat contradiction of our own knowledge of the man."

"How much do we know about him?"

"Well – ah – ah – the Immigration people must have checked his record before they accepted him. He did good service as a medical man in Lae. He's been very helpful over this malaria control business. It's not a great deal, of course, but – er –"

"No, it isn't."

"Dammit, man!" The Commissioner was suddenly and unreasonably angry. "What are you trying to do? Convict the man without evidence? I tell you there's a first-class scandal in this if ever –"

"I'm not trying to do anything," said George Oliver mildly. "I'm going up to investigate a situation that is reported to exist. Until I get there and look round I can't tell you what I'm going to do or even whether there is a situation at all. If you want a memo to that effect, I'll give it to you before I go. Is there anything else?"

The Commissioner was beaten but couldn't afford to admit it.

He said curtly, "No, there's nothing else. You'll want to get away this evening, of course. But I warn you, Oliver, if you make a mistake on this one, I'll have your head."

"I'll give it to you – on a chafing-dish."

George Oliver grinned sourly and went out. He had won a victory but it was as tasteless as the dust of defeat.

One hour and twenty minutes later he was slogging over the first foothills northward to Sonderfeld's valley. He reckoned it would take him two days to get there. The runner had made the trip in thirty-three hours; but George Oliver had to think of his heart and his arteries.

He was forty-five years old. He was beginning to feel his age.

Kurt Sonderfeld was beginning to feel the strain. His

126

plans had been laid a long time now, but as the day of their fulfilment approached he was conscious of a mounting tension, a thrusting eagerness that battered against the barriers of his habitual control. His project had been framed in isolation and retirement, now he was hemmed in by people, familiar but unfriendly, polite but mistrustful, whom his courtesy could not charm nor his cleverness wholly mystify.

Père Louis had stayed to breakfast and luncheon and dinner. He had slept a second night in the guest-room and taken his departure at first light the following morning. He had paid careful respect to the memory of Max Lansing, he had shared, solicitously, the grief of his friends. For the rest, he had refused to involve himself in discussions with Sonderfeld and had interested himself in the small problems of Gerda's garden, the gossip of the plantation, and the minor comedies of Curtis's census-taking.

Sonderfeld had tried, more than once, to re-open the question of the unrest in the valleys, but the old man refused to be drawn. There had been one rift between them. He did not care to risk another. Sonderfeld had the impression that the priest regretted his bluntness but dared not lose face by an open apology. His attitude to Gerda was one of solicitude and paternal interest in her feminine affairs. He wondered vaguely if Père Louis were trying to convert her to the Church.

He was glad to see the last of the canny old cleric.

The attitude of Lee Curtis troubled him even more. The boy was terse and abrupt, refusing all invitations to drink or share a meal as if he wished to be spared the demands of courtesy to a host whom he disliked. The Kiap house and the village – these were his domain and he kept to them religiously, as a monk to his cloisters.

Theodore Nelson was a different proposition. The round-faced Englishman was too seasoned a voyager to involve himself in the personal affairs of his company's clients. He made the rounds with Sonderfeld, talked

volubly and accurately of pest control and double crop-
ping and experimental strains and marketing problems;
but he was blankly disinterested in any but professional
subjects or the safe reminiscences of European exiles.
His thick spectacles were a visor that hid his wary eyes
and the fear that lurked behind them. He, too, was
warmer in his attentions to Gerda, more gentle in his
courtesy, more attentive to her quiet conversation. Sonderfeld asked himself if it were the beginning of a
new attachment. He would have welcomed it as a useful
diversion.

Gerda herself was as distant as the moon and just as
cold. If she grieved for the death of Lansing, she gave
no sign. If she suspected his own part in it, she made no
show of resentment. She kept his house and tended her
flowers and slept, unsmiling, the whole night through.
She had walled herself round with indifference and he
was not yet ready to lay seige to her defence.

It seemed to Sonderfeld that Wee Georgie was the
only one whose attitude towards him had not changed.
The gross old reprobate shuffled and wheezed around
him like a court jester, tattered and filthy in his motley,
full of bawdy tales and sly obscenities, fawning at his
frown, leering happily when Sonderfeld, for want of
better company, bent to his shabby slave. But when he
came to question him on his surveillance of N'Daria, Wee
Georgie's face went suddenly blank.

"There was nothin', boss. Nothin' at all I tell yer.
Twice she went up to the bungalow to draw rations.
That was all, the rest of the time she stayed in the
laboratory. True as Gawd she did."

"But the nights. What did she do then?"

"Same thing, boss. Stayed in the hut. Never stirred a
foot outside it."

Sonderfeld took hold of him by his shirt-front and
shook him till his face was purple and his eyes were
popping.

"You're lying to me, Georgie! Lying!"

"Why should I want to lie, boss?" Georgie choked and spluttered unhappily. "Why should I want to die?"

"Because you were drunk! Because you don't know what she did."

"Even suppose I were – which I weren't – me girls were awake, weren't they? Think they'd let her get out without knowin'? They went to the carry-leg every night, whoring down the village the way they always do. But she wasn't there. They'd have seen her if she was, wouldn't they? Ask 'em yourself, if you don't believe me."

The logic of it was sound enough, but Sonderfeld refused to accept it.

"Did anyone talk to her? The priest perhaps? Or Curtis or Nelson? Or my wife?"

"How could they boss? When she was in the hut the whole time. The missus might have had a few words with her when she went up to the house. But I doubt it. They haven't been speakin' for a while, have they? Anyway why ask me when you can get it from the girl herself? So help me, if I'm lyin' you can cut me liquor ration! I can't say better than that, now can I?"

"No, Georgie, you can't." Sonderfeld's lips parted in a thin smile. "And you know I'll do it, don't you? I'll have you screaming in torment in forty-eight hours. You know that, don't you?"

He turned on his heel and walked up the path towards the laboratory. Wee Georgie watched him go and licked his dry lips. Already he was regretting his offer to submit to trial by ordeal. His story was true as far as it went. The only part he hadn't told was the night when he and his two girls had huddled, cursing and scared, under the blanket listening to the footsteps of the cassowary bird and the low murmur of voices from the open door of the laboratory.

Half-way to the hut, Sonderfeld stopped to light a cigar. As he held the match, he noticed with surprise and irritation that his hand was trembling. He tossed away the match and stretched out his arm full length, his wrist rigid, splaying out his fingers like a fan. Still he could not control the tremor. He frowned and dropped his arm to his side.

He was disappointed in himself. Weakness like this was for other men, not for Kurt Sonderfeld. He was tired, of course. He had underestimated the pressures of the last few days. A small sedative and his nerves would be under control again. A sedative or – ?

He smiled at the simplicity of the diagnosis. He had not had a woman in a long time. He was a potent man; but he had been so busy with affairs of importance that he had ignored the needs of his nature. Gerda's coldness had helped him to continence and his desire for N'Daria had been tempered by his need to discipline her. Now she would serve him in a different fashion.

Slowly, and with infinite relish, he finished his cigar standing in the warm sunshine, surrendering himself to the soft, crawling itch of desire. He had worked hard, he had planned meticulously, he had gambled against the folly and blindness of inferior men. He had only to wait a little longer and the winnings would tumble into his lap. He needed pleasure and relaxation – there was a woman waiting to give him both. He tossed away the stub of his cigar and went into the laboratory.

The first sight of N'Daria shocked him deeply. Her eyes were puffy. Her skin was grey and tired. Her movements were slack and listless. When he greeted her, she answered him mechanically, her voice empty of resentment or pleasure, and bent again to her notes. He remembered the urgent, pleading youth of her and was faintly disappointed.

But desire was still strong in him and he flattered himself with the thought that he could make such ravages on a woman and still repair them with a touch of his hand. Softly, restraining his eagerness, he began to coax her. She shivered at his touch and tried to draw away,

130

but his grasp was too strong for her. She stiffened in revulsion, but he laughed softly and held her closer. Then slowly her body began to awaken and she was divided against herself.

Suddenly, she clung to him, urging him, native fashion, by beating her body against his own. Then he lifted her in his arms and carried her into the sleeping-room and made her teach him kunande and carry-leg, as if he were Kumo and she the bright and bird-like girl with the cane belt of courtship and the crown of green beetles and red feathers.

Spent at last, he lay beside her, wrapped in the soft, sad triumph of completion....

After a long while, he got up, dressed himself, and walked out into the laboratory without a word or a backward glance. When he stretched out his hand again it was as steady as a rock. He smiled and told himself that he was a sensible fellow who kept a wise balance between discipline and enjoyment.

He did not understand that Kurt Sonderfeld had already cracked under the strain.

CHAPTER 11

"ACHILLES...." Sonderfeld smiled tolerantly and pointed his cigar in the direction of the Kiap house. "Achilles is sulking in his tent. Unfortunately he is too young to make such gestures with any grace. He succeeds only in making himself ridiculous."

It was late in the afternoon – the afternoon of Oliver's departure from Goroka, the afternoon of his coupling with N'Daria. He was sitting on the stoop with Gerda and Nelson, relaxed, expansive, at ease with himself and his small world. Wee Georgie hovered in the background, shambling and solicitous.

The absence of Curtis was the only flaw in his pattern

131

of contentment. It was a small loss, to be sure. The boy was callow, uninformed, gauche. It was not his absence but his refusal to attend that fretted Sonderfeld. It was an affront to his hospitality, a small reverse in the lengthening tally of victories.

Gerda and Nelson said nothing, but watched him covertly over their drinks. Something had happened to the big man, but they could not put a name to it. His stringent control had slackened. His laugh was louder, his irritation more patent. His movements and his gestures were suddenly out of rhythm. The smooth-running machine was ever so little unbalanced, its beat was out of kilter, its bearings whined in protest.

Sonderfeld tossed off his drink and gestured to Wee Georgie to refill his glass. He turned to Nelson.

"Do you think, Nelson, it is because I have offended him?"

Nelson shrugged.

"Don't know. He hasn't said anything to me. He's very busy, of course."

"Busy! Busy!" His voice was harsh with anger and contempt. "A mission clerk could do in half a day what these fellows do with a dozen policemen and all the trappings of military authority. No, I will tell you what it is. It is one of the defects of the present system that sends these fellows – schoolboys most of them, half-trained, half-educated – into isolated areas and expects them to do a man's work. They are not prepared for it, mentally or physically. They are at an age when it is dangerous to live alone. They are armed with an authority beyond their strength. Small wonder that they become eccentric, cross-grained, a burden to themselves, a trial to those who are forced to have dealings with them."

Wee Georgie set a fresh drink at his elbow. Sonderfeld seized it and half emptied it at a gulp. Gerda watched him anxiously. She had never seen him like this before. She could deal with him sober, but drunk and out of control there was no knowing how dangerous he might be. She shivered and looked inquiringly at Theodore Nelson. The small, fluttering movement of his hand told her that he was helpless.

Then Wee Georgie caught her eye. He was standing behind Sonderfeld's chair and he jerked his thumb back and forth in the direction of the Kiap house. His meaning was plain. Gerda herself should go down and fetch Curtis.

Sonderfeld was frowning as he slipped the band off a new cigar and pierced the end with ritual care. His hands were trembling again and he fumbled uneasily with the small, sharp instrument. Gerda stood up. She masked her uneasiness with a cool smile and addressed herself to Theodore Nelson.

"If Kurt is right – and I think he may be – we should be gentle with the young man. We are the older ones. It is our business to make the first approaches. I'll go down and talk to Mr. Curtis myself."

Sonderfeld looked up sharply. Then his tight mouth relaxed into a smile of tolerant approval.

"Good! Good! If he will come, I am prepared to forget his bad manners and welcome him back into the circle. My wife has many defects, Nelson, but she has all the talents of a diplomat. Go, my dear, and charm Achilles into the sunlight. Georgie – drinks for Mr. Nelson and myself."

Gerda smoothed her skirts and patted her hair into place and walked swiftly down the path to the Kiap house. A small, icy finger of fear was probing at her heart.

Lee Curtis greeted her with surprise and pleasure and drew her into the cool half-light of the hut.

"Gerda! This is the nicest thing that's happened to me. What brings you here? Here, sit down. Make yourself comfortable."

The boyish warmth of his greeting touched her and

133

she was filled with tenderness towards him, young, lost and afraid, but stiffening his courage to a man's work in a harsh and alien country. She seated herself in the canvas chair, while he perched himself on an upturned box, eager and grateful for this small mark of her favour.

"I've been wanting to see you, Gerda. But I've had to keep away. I'm – I'm not very good at hiding my feelings and – well – it seemed safer."

"I know that. But now I want you to come."

"Why?"

"Because my husband is irritable, unsettled. Your absence annoys him. He's drinking more than he usually does."

"Oh!" His hurt was so obvious that it touched her to pity and she leant forward to lay a cool hand on his wrist.

"That isn't the only reason, believe me. I want you there, too. I'll be glad of your company. I won't be so afraid if you're there."

"Afraid of what?"

"I don't know. I wish I did. Kurt is changed. Always before he was so controlled, so much master of himself that nothing seemed to touch him. Now he is uneasy, restless. His whole manner is different. His voice is louder. He does not trouble to conceal his thoughts. I –"

"He's scared."

"Perhaps. But I am afraid, too. I know him so well, you see. I have seen the cruelty of which he is capable."

"Has he – been cruel to you?"

The young mouth tightened, the eyes were suddenly grim.

"No. But don't you see? It isn't that only. I am so isolated. When the pig festival comes, you will leave us and I shall be alone, completely alone. If Kurt succeeds in this crazy plan of his, what then?"

"I'll look after you, Gerda, I promise you."

Then he was at her side, his arms about her shoulders

134

in a protective gesture, his eyes tender, his lips brushing her cheeks. There was so much simple love in him that she had not the heart to reject him. He drew her to her feet and held her to him and kissed her lips and cradled her head awkwardly on his shoulder. She was warm to him, but there was no passion in her response and she drew away as quickly as she could.

He pleaded with her.

"I love you, Gerda. You know that now, don't you? You understand that I won't let anything happen to you. We've got more than half a case against your husband now and when George Oliver comes up –"

The words were out before he remembered that this was to be a secret between himself and Nelson and Père Louis. Gerda's face went grey; her mouth dropped open; her eyes stared blankly. Her voice was a frightened whisper.

"George Oliver?"

"That's right. He's the A.D.O. at Goroka. He's my boss. It was to be a secret, but I don't see that it matters if you know. Père Louis and I sent reports to him. He's probably on his way now.... I say, are you sick? You look awful."

"No, no! I'm all right. Just let me sit down and give me a drink of water."

He settled her solicitously in the chair and turned away to fill a mug from the canvas water-bag hanging in the doorway. Gerda closed her eyes and tried vainly to marshal her scattered thoughts.

George Oliver! One love remembered from the many now forgotten. One warmth remembered out of all the cold and barren years. The one regret from all the loveless laughter. Now he was coming back – not for her, but for her husband. She remembered his brooding eyes and his hurt mouth and the droop of his tired shoulders when he turned away for the last time.

"Drink this. It'll make you feel better."

Lee Curtis was squatting beside the chair offering the

pannikin of water like a lover's token. She sipped it slowly, veiling his eyes from him lest he should read his own rejection before she had time to prepare him for it.

"Thank you, my dear. I am better now."

He took the tin cup from her hands and moved away a pace or two to set it on the table. When he came back, she was standing up, smoothing her frock, patting her hair with the old, familiar, intimate gesture. He watched her, puzzled and half afraid. Then she took his hands in hers and spoke softly and with compassion.

"Lee, you have paid me a very great compliment. I shall remember it all my life. But I am not for you. I am too old, for one thing. For another, I know that I could never make you happy. No, listen to me, please –" He opened his mouth to speak but she closed it with the palm of her cool hand. "You are too young to bind your life to that of a woman who has lived as I have. I have loved many men. I am married to a man I hate. The burden of a past like that would crush you and you would come to hate me. I could not bear that. Besides ..." Now, she knew she must say it, as much for herself as for him. She might deny it later, she probably would, but here in the shadows of the Kiap house she must make affirmation of the last shred of faith left to her. "Besides, I am in love with George Oliver."

For a long time he stood there, head drooping, his body slack, his hands plucking helplessly at the seams of his trousers. When at last he straightened up, his mouth was twisted into a tremulous youthful grin.

"Well, that's it. I daresay I can take it, given time. Now wait till I spruce up and I'll drink myself silly on your husband's grog."

He douched his face and straightened his hair, changed his shirt and buckled on his belt, and then walked with her back to the bungalow. His heart was empty and his brain was tired; he felt like a man who had wakened suddenly from a nightmare and groped frantically for a hand-hold on reality. But his back was straight and his head was high and he greeted Kurt Sonderfeld with a smile.

Cadet Patrol Officer Lee Curtis had entered into man's estate.

Once again they were dining together in the candlelit room with its vista of stars and dark mountains, while the kundus thundered up from the valley and the chant rose and fell into crests and hollows of melody. Once again there was the warmth of wine and the savour of fine food and the smell of flowers and the shifting play of flames on silver and crystal.

But there were ghosts at the banquet – the ghost of Max Lansing, querulous, demanding, disappointed, inescapable; the crackling echo of Père Louis' voice, interpreting the signs and the portents; the monstrous tossing shadow of Kumo the Sorcerer, symbol of all the dark evil of the valleys. There were ghosts at the banquet and their presence could not be ignored, their voices could not be stifled.

The talk eddied uneasily round the quartet at the table, lapsed and stirred again as Sonderfeld, flushed and emphatic, commanded their attention to a new subject or an old argument. He had been drinking deeply and steadily since the end of the afternoon and he was by turn truculent and goading, or given to fantastic condescensions and wild laughter. Gerda was shocked and helpless, afraid to provoke him, ashamed for herself and her guests. Theodore Nelson kept his eyes on his plate and tried vainly to escape the attention of his host. But Sonderfeld nagged at him with perverse amusement and soon reduced him to mumbling confusion.

Then he turned his attention to Lee Curtis. His big voice boomed in drunken mockery.

"Now, Curtis, you are among friends. You can afford to be frank. Tell me, have you never found yourself tempted to try the village women?"

"Kurt, please –"

"No, my dear, you must not be prudish. It does not become you. Mr. Curtis is a man of the world – even if a very young one. He lives much alone. He would be the first to admit his need of the satisfactions of the flesh. Well, my friend?"

Curtis flushed with anger but he kept a tight hold on himself.

He said, coldly, "So far I haven't been interested."

"Yet some of them are beautiful, are they not? Scrape off the pig fat, take the lice out of their hair, wash them well with soap and water, don't you think they would grace your bed as well as – say, Gerda here."

"I – I – I say old man. . . ." Nelson began to stammer a half-hearted protest.

Curtis cut him short with a gesture.

"If you'll leave your wife's name out of it, Sonderfeld, I'll answer your question."

"Forgive me!" Sonderfeld waved a regal hand. "I offend you. I mentioned Gerda simply for comparison. She is beautiful, is she not? I believe other men find her desirable. I did myself once. However, we will omit her from the proposition. You will admit that in certain circumstances dark flesh might be very desirable?"

"Possibly."

"To you?"

"I doubt it."

"And yet there are cases on record of – shall we call them lapses – even among your own colleagues."

"Not within my experience."

"But then," Sonderfeld's voice dropped to a low purring pitch of calculated insult, "you are so very young, Curtis. Your experience is so very limited. How can you say what the years may do to you? How can you promise that you will not sicken of hot-house fruit and turn to the wild vine and the apples of Sodom? What would you say if I told you that I, myself, have tasted them and found them sweet?"

"I would remind you," said Curtis, bluntly, "that it's

an offence against Territory law to cohabit with native women. I'd also remind you that you've had too much to drink. I suggest it time you started to sleep it off."

"*Gott im Himmel!*" Sonderfeld crashed his fist on the table top, so that the glass shattered and the cutlery danced and rattled under the flickering candle flames. "In my own house, at my own table, I am reprimanded by a puppy!"

"I didn't ask to come," said Curtis quietly. "I didn't expect to be insulted."

"No, that's true."

As suddenly as it had come, his anger seemed to leave him. His features composed themselves into a mask of smiling approbation. Ignoring the wreckage on the table, he leant forward in the attitude of a great gentleman delivering a careful compliment.

"You know, Curtis, I like you. You have more brains than I gave you credit for. You have courage, too. Do you never feel that you are wasted in this pitiful routine – poking through the valleys, sitting in judgement on childish disputes, listening to childish lies, making little lists of folk who will be dead in two years, writing reports that no one ever reads?"

"No, I don't."

"But you are, you know. Look!" He slewed round, unsteadily, in his chair and flung his arm out in a forensic attitude towards the broad view window that framed the stars and the black barrier of the mountains. "Out there is the last unknown country on the map of the world. Behind those mountains there is wealth undreamed of, gold and oil and manpower, to turn this wilderness into a paradise. There are a million men in the valleys waiting for a leader, ten thousand drums waiting to burst into the march of the conqueror. And you have – what? Ten thousand Europeans and a shabby charter from United Nations. Look at it, man! Look and look again and tell me whose way is right – yours or mine?"

"What is your way, Sonderfeld?"

The question was soft and innocent but it had the impact of a bullet. Sonderfeld's hieratic attitude was gone in an instant. His face twisted into a grin; his eyes were cunning and wary as an animal.

"Oh, no, Curtis! I am not so big a fool! Why should I peddle my visions to the blind and shout my message to the deaf? Go back to your hut! Suck your pencil-stub and scribble your little notes and wait for the thunder and the lightning that will strike you dead!"

He heaved himself from his chair and lurched unsteadily to the door. Then he turned and looked at them. His face was distorted, his lips slobbered, his eyes were sullen and bloodshot. His voice was hoarse with liquor and excitement.

"The cassowary men are abroad in the valleys. They run from village to village with the news of the great coming. There is a name spoken that is louder than the drums. There is a chief promised who will raise the tribute of the valleys, who will sweep from the Sepik to the Huon Gulf and the name of the chief is – is –"

He broke off. He seemed suddenly to understand where he was and what he was saying. They saw him struggling for control, shaking his head to clear it of the liquor fumes, composing his flushed features into a travesty of smiling charm. He steadied himself against the door-jamb and surveyed them with something of the old mockery. Then he made them a little bow and left them. They heard him stumbling out on to the verandah, down the steps and on to the path that led to the laboratory.

Then they looked at each other with relief and with horror, and in the eyes of each was the same unspoken verdict.

Gerda buried her face in her hands and sobbed. Lee Curtis patted her shoulder awkwardly and made a sign to Nelson to wait for him on the verandah. He hesitated

140

a moment, as if unwilling to be left alone, then he went out, polishing his glasses, peering anxiously into the shadows as if afraid that Sonderfeld might be waiting to leap upon him out of the darkness.

Slowly, painfully, Gerda recovered herself. She dried her eyes on Curtis's handkerchief and took the cigarette that he offered her. She smoked a few moments in silence until her hands stopped trembling and her tight nerves began to relax. Then she turned to him with a simple, pathetic question.

"What am I going to do, Lee? Tell me, please."

"Wait. That's all you can do. Wait till George Oliver gets here."

"But Kurt . . . ? You saw him. What . . . ?"

"He was drunk. He'll sober up before morning."

"He was mad. You know that as well as I do."

"There's no one here to certify him, Gerda."

"But what am I to do?" It was a cry of terror wrung from her by the sudden press of memories she had thought buried for ever – memories of Rehmsdorf and the gas-chambers and the protracted torment of the damned and the dispossessed.

"Nothing. Nelson and I will stay here tonight, in the guest-room. You've only to raise your voice and we'll come running. Besides, he may not even come back. He may decide to sleep it off in the laboratory."

She saw him then with new eyes. She saw him tempered, as steel is tempered, violently and abruptly in fire and water, to a new strength and hardness. The soft lines of youth had disappeared. His mouth and his eyes were hard and the skin of his cheeks was tight as vellum on a drum. This was what must have happened to George Oliver – this and things like it – until youth was dead and there were no illusions left and the heart was empty of all but strength.

She came to him then and took his face in her hands and kissed him gently on the lips, and though he knew that she was kissing another man he did not resent it. He took her arm and led her out on to the verandah where Theodore Nelson was waiting for them.

For all his huckster's shrewdness, for all the bright burnish that travel had given him, the round-faced, myopic fellow was of indifferent courage. He drove hard bargains for the men who stood behind him in business. He made profit for scant payment in the casual commerce of the bed. His mind was a card-index of facts and figures and dossiers of people who might be useful to him. He was amusing when he cared to be, brusque and inconsiderate when his comfort or convenience were involved. He had travelled the world in pursuit of one star, apparently unaware that it was a gaudy pasteboard pinned to his own navel. Inside, he was as hollow as a coconut.

He had made his alliance with Lee Curtis, because despite his youth, the patrol officer represented the big battalions. Now, when the treaty seemed to demand service in return for protection, he wanted to dissolve it as soon as possible. Sitting alone in the darkness, listening to the beat of the drums, he had framed his proposition with some care. Now he laid it before Lee Curtis.

"Have you told Mrs. Sonderfeld about the – er – arrangements?"

"About Oliver coming up? Yes. There was no good reason why she shouldn't hear about it."

"Good. When do you expect Oliver to get here?"

"Late tomorrow, possibly. More than likely the following morning."

"Will he be bringing more police with him?"

"I should think so. Depends on what's available in the pool at Goroka. Why?"

"Well – er – I have a very tight schedule, as you know. Lots of places still to see in the Territory. Then I have to get back to Sydney to catch a ship for Colombo –"

"Yes?"

The monosyllable wasn't encouraging, but Theodore Nelson stuck to his script.

"Well, I'm not much use to you here. This sort of fandango isn't my choice of entertainment. So I thought – er – with Oliver on the way, you'd be able to give me a couple of police-boys for escort back to Goroka. I could leave first thing in the morning."

"You could leave tonight."

"Well, there's not that much hurry. But of course, if you thought . . ."

"You want to know what I think, Nelson?"

"What?"

Curtis's voice was a savage lash of anger and contempt.

"I think you're a yellow-livered bastard. So far as I'm concerned you can get out any time you like – alone!"

"You have a duty to protect me. That's the understanding on which the company . . ."

"You're being protected. You're sitting on this veranda with your belly full of food and whisky. What more do you want?"

"There's trouble blowing up. If you can't guarantee my safety, then I demand to be sent back under escort."

"I can't spare an escort. Besides, the southern tracks are as safe as King's Cross – a damn' sight safer, come to that. The trouble's up there, fifteen, twenty miles north. You'll be going the other way. I'll give you two days' rations and you can sleep in the Kiap houses. That's the best I can do. Make up your own mind."

Before Nelson had time to frame his reply, the drums stopped abruptly. The sudden silence was as commanding as a trumpet blast. Tense, expectant, they peered out across the valley. They saw no movement. Even the trees and the feathery bamboos hung still in the windless air. Then, distant but distinct, they heard the crescendo beat of the running cassowary.

"What's that?" Gerda whispered the question close to Curtis's ear.

"Cassowary," said Curtis flatly.

"Kumo?"

"Probably."

"What do you mean – Kumo?" Nelson's voice was a husky croak. "A man doesn't run like that. He couldn't."

"I know," said Curtis quietly.

"Then what the devil . . . ?"

Curtis was silent a moment as if debating whether to answer. When he spoke it was with a sort of calculated calm.

"I can't tell you very much, because I don't know. It's common belief among the tribes that certain sorcerers have the power to change themselves into cassowaries and travel between the villages faster than a man could possibly run. I've heard accounts from reliable men, old hands, missionaries, that point to such things actually happening. I've never heard one who was prepared to deny it flatly. Two things I do know." He paused a moment, listening to the drumming crescendo. "The first is that that's a cassowary out there. And yet . . . the cassowary never travels at night."

"What does it mean?"

"I don't know. I've half a mind to go down and find out."

"No, please !" Gerda clung to him desperately. "You can't leave us here. It's your duty to protect us."

"Oh, for God's sake, Nelson !"

For a few moments he sat, undecided whether to go or stay, then he decided with some relief that there would be little profit and possibly a great loss in an abortive effort to confront the sorcerer. Even if he succeeded, what could he say or do? Sonderfeld was the man he wanted and already Sonderfeld had played half-way into his hands. He relaxed in his chair, lit two cigarettes, handed one to Gerda, and listened to the steady chuff-chuff-chuff of the great earth-bound bird that never travelled at night.

When they reached the village, the footbeats stopped

and for twenty minutes or more there was silence, broken only by the small crepitant noises of the night and the low murmur of their own desultory talk. Then, from down in the village, came a wild shout of triumph whose echoes rang startlingly across the sleeping valley. Then the drums broke out again, and the singing – a new rhythm and a new chant, savage, exultant, rolling like thunder round the ridges and the peaks.

"To hell with it!" said Lee Curtis. "Let's go to bed. We share the guest-room, Nelson. Four-hour watches. If Gerda calls, wake me immediately."

"You can't give me orders like that!" Nelson's voice was high and petulant.

"I give 'em, you take 'em. If not, you spend the night in the Kiap house – alone. Come on, Gerda, you've had enough for tonight. It won't look half so bad in the morning."

Together they walked into the house with Theodore Nelson at their heels like a frightened puppy. At the door of her room, she kissed him lightly and left him.

He went straight to the guest-room and flung himself, fully dressed, in the arm-chair, leaving Theodore Nelson to sleep the first four hours of the night-watch.

At two in the morning, Sonderfeld had still not returned, so he woke Nelson and sat him, grumbling and ill-tempered, in the chair, while he himself stretched out on the bed for a few hours of uneasy slumber.

But Nelson was a man who needed his rest. He nodded and dozed fitfully and finally slept, forgetting even to awake Curtis to relieve him.

When morning came, they found that Sonderfeld was gone, taking N'Daria with him, and that the whole village was moving out to the pig festival.

CHAPTER 12

THEY poured out of the valley like an army on the march.

Plumed and painted, armed with stone axes and clubs and bows and arrows, the warriors strode out to the beat of the black kundus. Their marching song was a long repetitive ululation, counterpointed to the pattern of the snake-skin drums. The sound echoed and re-echoed till it hung like a moving haze of melody along the shoulders of the mountains.

Behind the warriors came the unmarried girls dressed in their finery, their blood pulsing in time with the kundus, their flesh fired by the sight of the sweating male bodies rippling and swaying in the stamping gait of the march. Between them were the pigs – some carried trussed on long poles, others leashed and led like dogs, while the laughing, screaming children prodded them with sticks to urge them to greater speed. They grunted and snuffled and squealed and the sound was a new theme in the wild orchestration of the tribal triumph.

Then came the married women, old and young, their bodies bowed under the weight of suckling children and huge string baskets filled with taro and paw-paws and bananas. They, too, were decked in unaccustomed finery, with necklets of green snailshell and pubic skirts of fresh taro leaves. They giggled and gossiped and took up the refrain in short breathless bursts of song. For them the pig festival was a rare release from the domestic slavery into which they had lapsed when their kunande days were over and they shed the cane belt and the ornaments of courtship.

The procession wound through the defiles like a long, bright snake. It formed into a solid, shouting phalanx when they broke out of the jungle into broad patches of kunai grass, and drummed up the rises onto the high spine of the ranges. They were the last to come to the assembly of the tribes. It was part of their pride to make an impressive entrance into the broad, green crater of the Lahgi Valley.

When they topped the final rise they halted and reassembled and looked down into the broad, rich basin that was the cradle of their race. Here was the spreading village of the tribe paramount, grown now to double its normal size, with new huts and long kunande houses for the reception of the guests. Here were the broad taro plots, criss-crossed by the sluggish runnels of the irrigation ditches. There was the long formal avenue of the dancing place and at the end of it, a great palisade pen of casuarina wood to hold the pigs that would be slaughtered at the festival.

The village was alive with plumed and painted figures, misty with the smoke of a hundred cooking-fires, and murmurous with the gossip of a dozen valleys. A small knot of elders was moving towards the main entrance of the compound, ready to offer formal welcome to the last-comers and receive the pigs and the taro that were their tribute to the festival.

When the watchers on the hill caught sight of them, they set up a great shout that rang and echoed round the crater rim, to be answered by another cry that drifted up from the village like a wind. Then the luluai gave a sharp command. The drummers dressed their ranks, the warriors hefted their axes and their clubs. The women took a tight grip on their children and their baskets. The unmarried hoisted the pig poles on their shoulders and waited.

There was a moment of tense silence. Then the drums broke out, and the singing – a mighty roar that crashed like thunder over the valley as the plumed and painted army rolled down the green slope to the meeting of the tribes.

Lee Curtis stood on the verandah of Sonderfeld's bungalow and stared across the empty valley. Gerda was with him, and Nelson, and Wee Georgie. Below him, on the lawn, the police-boys were drawn up waiting the order to march. It was three in the afternoon. The silence and the emptiness were strange to them – strange and frightening after the disciplined activity of the normal plantation days. There were no labourers among the coffee rows. The new clearing was deserted. There was no smoke from the village. No chattering garden-boys clipped the lawns or raked the river-gravel on the paths. Even the house-boys had left them, and the bungalow was a hollow echoing shell.

Curtis finished his cigarette and flicked the stub over the bamboo rail. Then he gave them his final instructions.

"You'll stay around the house until Oliver arrives. He may come tonight. Personally, I don't expect him till tomorrow morning, I don't think you'll have any trouble – in fact I'm sure you won't – but, just in case, I want you to stay together. Understand?"

The others nodded agreement but said nothing. On the face of it, what was there to say?

Curtis continued briskly.

"You'll sleep at the house, Nelson. Same with you, Georgie – and lay off the liquor or I'll run you in on a charge of sleeping with tribal women!"

Wee Georgie grinned and tugged his shaggy forelock.

"I'm leaving you one rifle and fifty rounds. That's all I can spare. Gerda, you'll look after that."

Nelson flushed at the snub, but made no reply.

"When Oliver comes, tell him I've gone up to the Lahgi Valley. I'm picking up Père Louis on the way and we'll camp tonight on the lip of the crater. I'll wait for him there, unless they turn on the big ceremony sooner than I expect. In that case, I'll move into the village. Is that clear?"

"I'll tell him," said Gerda simply. "Is there anything else?"

"No. That's the lot. Take it easy and don't worry. Whatever happens will be twenty miles away. I count on having it under control before you hear a whisper back here."

"Er – care for a drink before you go, Mr. Curtis?" said Wee Georgie, licking his dry lips.

"No thanks, Georgie. I'm on duty."

He grinned boyishly, hitched up his pistol belt and held out his hand to Gerda.

"Good luck, Gerda. Good luck with Oliver, too."

"Good luck, and thank you, Lee."

Ignoring Nelson's offered hand and, with a friendly pat on Wee Georgie's drooping shoulder, he left them and walked swiftly down the steps to the lawn.

The police-boys snapped to attention. The fuzzy-wuzzy sergeant came to the salute. Curtis barked an order. They shouldered arms like guardsmen and the next moment saw them striding down the path – a tiny army of black-skinned mercenaries, led by a stripling boy.

Gerda Sonderfeld stood watching them until they disappeared in the turning of the valley, then without a word she walked into the house and shut herself in the bedroom.

Wee Georgie stuck his thumbs in his string belt and puffed out his belly like a great, happy toad.

"What would you say to a drink – eh, Mr. Nelson?"

George Oliver was still plugging over the high saddles of the southward ranges. He was making good time. He expected to arrive in Sonderfeld's valley shortly before midnight. He grinned wryly as he remembered his constant lectures to the young patrol officers on the costly folly of forced marches. If they had to meet trouble, they should meet it fresh. Tired men make mistakes of judgement and timing. Weary bodies fall easy prey to the parasitic infections of the wild valleys.

His own body was bone tired. Weariness was lead in

149

his marrows and a stink on his brown, sweating skin. His feet were swollen in his soft boots and his throat was parched like a lime-pit. As he walked, he rinsed his mouth with water and spat the residue on the ground. That was another lesson in his syllabus. A tired man cannot march with liquid slopping around in his stomach.

He looked round at the police-boys and the cargo-carriers. They were dragging their feet with weariness, panting with effort to match his steady slogging pace. He was driving them as hard as he was driving himself – but they were loaded with packs and rifles while he had his shoulders free.

When they dropped down into the shadows of a narrow valley and came to the edge of a small creek, he halted them for a brief rest. They slipped off their packs, laid their rifles against a rock, and threw themselves flat on their bellies, scooping up the water with their cupped hands.

George Oliver sat propped against the rock-face and smoked a cigarette.

Times like these, he thought, were the happiest of his life. He was alone, master of himself and of the situation of the moment. He need not defer to the opinions of the uninformed, nor bend to the pressures of the diplomats and the politicos. Success was sweeter because it was seasoned with his own sweat. Even failure was bearable when it came from the strength of the opposition and not from the folly of colleagues or the blindness of superiors.

But a man could not always be alone. The time would come when his strength would fail him and he would be forced to turn to the comfort of a community in which he had no firm place, the support of friendships, rare in his lonely life. It was easier when a man was married. There was love and companionship, sometimes a family. There was a pride of possession and a place of refuge. There was the small but decent kingship of his own household.

So, by inevitable conjunction, his thought came back to Gerda Sonderfeld.

He knew now that he still loved her. Else why was he driving himself on this crazy, breakneck march over the mountains? He had travelled slower to more urgent meetings than this with Père Louis and Lee Curtis. He could, if he chose, make camp for the night and still arrive in time for the critical performance of the pig festival. What else but love compelled him to the final trial of her heart and his own, to the abasement of the beggar and the imminent despair of the rejected?

He hoisted himself stiffly to his feet, shouted an order to the boys, and stood over them while they loaded the packs and adjusted the webbing straps for the last, stiff haul. Then he grinned at them and jerked his thumb towards the farther hills.

"Come! We will show the mountain men how we can march."

Soon they were back into the plodding rhythm of the road, and the dusty paths were falling away beneath them while the shadows lengthened and the slow chill of the mountains crept into their bones.

When they came to the last great shoulder that stood like a black sentinel on the southern limit of Sonderfeld's domain, Oliver called another halt. The stars hung low in the velvet arch of the sky – so low and so bright it seemed he had only to reach up and pluck them like silver fruit. There was no moon. The air was keen as a knife blade, and he shivered as the chill struck him after the warm exertion of the trek.

The boys squatted on the ground, glad of the respite, chewing betel nut and asking themselves whether the Kiap would let them rest in the valley or whether he would thrust them farther into the dark and tedious mountains. The Kiap was a hard man and an ill one to cross. Their eyes followed him as he walked to the edge of the plateau and stood looking down at the broad valley, locked between the black arms of the mountains.

He saw it first as a dark and brooding pool refusing even the reflection of the cold stars. He heard it first as a silence, for there were no drums and the singers were far away. He felt it as an emptiness, from which even the pungent smoke of the village fires was long since blown away and lost. Then he saw the light – a tiny yellow pin-point, far away at the bottom of the shadowy lake. It was so small, so faint and pitiful, that it moved him almost to tears – as if it were a star at the bottom of a well, or a last brave hope in the black desert of despair.

The tribes had left the valley. He had come later than he wished, to assert the authority of the Kiap law. There was a light in the bungalow. Gerda was there. He asked himself with sour irony whether he had come too late for love.

Then, because he was a tidy fellow, he put the thought away and set himself to consider the situation in the light of Curtis's report and his own knowledge. The villagers had moved out. They always moved at sunrise, so they had been gone at most two days – possibly only one. If the villagers were gone, Sonderfeld was gone also, since the success of his project depended on his presence at the festival.

Curtis would have moved out. Père Louis would be waiting in his own village. That left Wee Georgie, the coffee fellow – whatever his name was – and Gerda. Two men and a woman waiting for the curtain to rise on a primitive drama of ambition, sorcery and lust.

To hell with it! He was dramatizing the situation to make it fit his mood – a dangerous luxury which had brought more than one luckless fellow an arrow in the guts or a stone axe crashing into his skull.

He called the boys to their feet and together they walked down the long winding path that led to the tiny yellow light in the centre of the valley.

Wee Georgie was drunk and snoring on the verandah.

Theodore Nelson tossed restlessly behind the locked door of the guest-room. Gerda Sonderfeld sat alone in the lamplight and waited for George Oliver to arrive.

In spite of Lee Curtis's warning not to expect him before morning, the conviction was strong in her that he would come that same night. It was as if she were plotting the stages for him, willing him to be at this point or that in time to make the final landfall before midnight. It was a folly and she knew it, just as it was a folly to expect love to survive the shock of such humiliation as she had inflicted on George Oliver – not a boy, like Lee Curtis – but a lonely, tired man with a bitter strength and a perverse dignity. It was a folly, too, to believe that after so much profanation in the name of love, she herself could ever come to the enjoyment of the fruits of love. Love – so simple a reality to which others came, effortless, unknowing, but, for herself, a peak beyond attainment. Folly! Yet what was left to her but folly, with Kurt raving after his crazy crown, and Curtis gone, and Père Louis solicitous for the needs of his own flock so that he had little time for the lost, contrary lamb still bleating in the dark desert? What was left but folly and folly's dream to rest her heart on as she dozed over the table top and waited for George Oliver to come?

She woke to the sound of his footsteps on the verandah, and when she leapt up, in sudden fear, she saw him standing in the doorway.

"Hullo, Gerda!"

"George! Thank God!"

Her heart cried out to him, but she stood motionless as a statue. She saw him, rocking with weariness, his face lined and haggard, his eyes bloodshot, his clothes dusty and stained with sweat – and yet her feet would not carry her to him and her slack hands were empty of comfort.

For a long moment he stood looking at her, drooping and tired, then he straightened up and his voice was dry with dust and fatigue.

153

"When did the tribe move out?"

"This morning."

"Where's Curtis?"

"Left this afternoon. He's picking up Père Louis. They'll wait for you on the lip of the crater. He said –"

"Where's your husband?"

"Gone."

"When?"

"Early this morning. He's mad, George. We think he left with Kumo and –"

"That's all I need to know for the present."

He stood a moment, eyes closed, weighing the facts, then apparently satisfied, he relaxed once more. He lurched into the room, pulled out a chair and sat down heavily.

"Have you got a drink? I'm dog tired." He grinned wearily, brushing his grey face with the back of his hand. "Fifty miles in thirty-eight hours. Not bad for an old stager."

She came to him then – came with little running steps from the far side of table. She wanted to throw her arms around him and kiss him on the lips and on his tired eyes, but she dared not. Instead she took off his slouch hat and unfastened the webbing pistol belt and knelt to loosen the boots from his swollen blistered feet. He suffered the service with the thankless resignation of a man too tired to care. He was slumped across the table, head pillowed on his arms, his breath coming in long sobbing gasps. She laid a tentative hand on his dusty greying hair, but if he felt it he gave no sign.

She brought him whisky and soda and watched while he drank two stiff drinks in succession and sat silently till the slow, illusory strength flowed back into his body.

"Thanks," he said flatly. "Thanks, I needed that."

"Have you eaten, George?"

He nodded absently.

"On the road. I've told my fellows to camp in your boy-houses, do you mind?"

"Of course not. You – You're staying then?"

She tried to conceal her eagerness, but her voice was shaky and she stammered over the question. He answered in the same flat listless voice.

"Yes, I'll sleep the night here and push off in the morning. Nothing will happen till the day after tomorrow."

"Are you sure of that?"

"Yes. The big ceremony comes last of all. There's a ritual of preparation first."

"Lee Curtis seemed to think –"

"Lee Curtis is new. He doesn't know everything."

His voice was edged with irritation. Without waiting for an invitation, he splashed another drink into his glass and drank, more slowly this time. Then he set it down, half finished, and lifted his eyes, studying her feature by feature as if seeing her for the first time.

Now, she thought, it would come – the tired mockery, the knife pricking at the one tender spot in her heart, the pressure on the hilt, slow and calculated, the blade sliding in, the brief but final agony before love was slain and faith and hope died with it. Silent and rigid, she sat with downcast eyes, waiting. When he spoke, his voice seemed to come from a great distance.

"You'd better give me the whole story. The reports I got were pretty scrappy."

So the execution was to be deferred. George Oliver was a good official. He would postpone his private pleasures until the business of the state was dispatched. She felt no relief – only a chill calm. She raised her eyes, and saw that he was lighting a cigarette and that his hands were unsteady. He pushed the packet across to her.

"Have one yourself."

"Thanks."

He did not offer her a light, so she reached across for the matchbox, lit up, pushed the box back across the shining table top and smoked for a few moments while she collected her thoughts.

Then she told him.

So that he would understand fully, so that there would be no doubt at all in his mind when he came to the moment of execution, she told him from the beginning – the far beginning when Sonderfeld was Reinach and Gerda was Gerda Rudenko and there was still hope in the world and love had not yet become a folly-fire beyond the stretch of her fingers.

As she talked, he smoked and drank, sitting slackly in the chair, his chin sunk on his chest, his eyes closed as if in sleep. But he was not sleeping. When she told him of N'Daria and Kumo and Lansing and Père Louis and Sonderfeld's final madness at the dinner-table, he became alert, questioning her closely on detail after detail, while his eyes darkened and his tired mouth stiffened into a thin line. Then at last her story was finished.

"That's all, George. I have no secrets left."

That was what her voice said; but her heart was crying, "Now you know everything. There is no spice lacking to the enjoyment of the triumph. I am bound and blindfolded – at least let the execution be swift."

Now he was looking at her again, measuring her with brooding eyes, like a gambler calculating the odds on his final, fateful throw.

Then he spoke.

"I've got one more question."

"Yes?"

He waited a long moment, then, one by one he laid the words down like chips on a green baize table top.

"I told you once I loved you. I still do. If – if you could be free of Sonderfeld, would you marry me?"

The next moment she was in his arms, crying, laughing, sobbing in a wild ecstacy of relief.

"Oh, God! Oh God in heaven! Yes! Yes! Yes!"

CHAPTER 13

GEORGE OLIVER groaned and mumbled and tossed uneasily in his sleep. Gerda sat up in bed and looked across at him in the half-light. He was lying on his back, one hand under his head, the other extended and plucking spasmodically at the covers. His lean face was still unrested, and his naked breast rose and fell in the gasping, unsteady rhythm of the nightmare.

Pity and love and desire welled up in her and she longed to go to him, settle him to calm again and lie beside him in the narrow bed until the first sunburst broke over the ridge and flowed down into the valley.

Yet she dared not touch him.

Once, in the old time together, she had awakened him out of such a nightmare and he had sat up instantly, eyes staring, his mouth full of wild curses, while his hands throttled the first scream of terror in her throat. Then he had warned her – tenderly, regretfully.

"Never do it, sweetheart! Never waken me like that. Just call me. If you must touch me, stand at the head of the cot out of reach of my hands."

"But why? In heaven's name, why?"

She was hurt and frightened and more than a little angry. He was gravely apologetic.

"Because, my dear, when you live the life I do, you sleep like Damocles under the hanging sword – only in my case it's a stone axe or a twelve-pound club. You wake at the slightest movement and your instinctive reaction is to defend yourself. It's a good reaction. It's saved by life more than once; but" – he grinned ironically – "I understand its damned uncomfortable to live with."

She lay there now with the memory of that other night and watched him with love and loneliness.

157

She understood now what this country did to men like George Oliver. It gave them fungoid ulcers and infective tinea and swollen spleens and scrub typhus. It thinned their blood and honed the youth out of their bodies and gave them nightmares, peopled with plumed monsters, haunted with savage drums, nightmares whose end was death and a grave without an epitaph.

And yet they loved the Territory and its peoples – loved it with the shamefaced passion of a lover for a fickle mistress, of a husband for a thankless, contrary wife.

They had no part or possession in the land, as Kurt had, or the settlers along the Highland road, or the shrewd business men from the south, with their saw-mills and their pulping factories and their holdings in gold and transport and the big earth-moving enterprises.

These were the rootless ones, the unrewarded and the unremembered, the first to come, the last to go, despised by the hucksters, resented by the exploiters, unthanked by the tribes whose women they kept clean, whose taro patch they held inviolate. These were the officials in exile, wards of the outer march, poorest yet proudest of all the proconsuls.

George Oliver stirred again, wrestling with his pillow, tugging the white sheet up around his shoulders. Then, quite suddenly, the nightmare left him and he relaxed, breathing as regularly as a sleeping child, while the corners of his mouth twitched upward into a smile.

Her heart warmed to him and her body, too, and she smiled at him across the narrow gap that separated them. She remembered all the other nights – and asked herself whether this was not the sweetest of all, passionless and celibate though it was.

For the short, wild moments after the revelation they had clung to each other; then, when they drew apart, George Oliver had grinned at her boyishly.

"Time for bed, sweetheart. I'll take a shower and turn in."

"I'll get the bed ready."

"Oh – er – Gerda?"

"Darling?"

He tilted up her chin and kissed her lightly.

"I couldn't make love to the Queen of Sheba tonight. Besides, I'll be wearing your husband's pyjamas."

She was instantly serious. She caught at his shirt and drew him to her and laid her head on his breast so that he could not see the shame in her eyes, nor the fear that he might reject her in this final moment.

"George, let me say something."

"Make it short, my dear. I'm dead on my feet."

"It will be short. I love you, darling, I need you, desire you, but I don't want you until I can come to you as your wife, without concealment, without all the shame of the old years. From a woman like me, perhaps, that is too much a folly to be borne. But at this moment, I feel it is what I wish."

"Good. I feel the same way. Now, please –" He disengaged himself, gently. "Please, let's get some sleep."

She led him to the bedroom and helped him to undress and fussed about him with soap and towels and clean pyjamas – and was happier than she had been in her whole life.

Now, in the dull darkness that comes before the false dawn, when life is at its lowest ebb, and happiness is a small unsteady candle, she sat watching her sleeping lover and seeing, as if for the first time, all the things that must be done, all the wild miracles that must come to pass, before their joy was half-way complete.

First, the tribes must be brought to discipline, the unrest among them stifled before it broke into a bloody madness, spilling through the network of the high valleys. Easy to say, easy to record in the dry and dusty phrases of a patrol report. But there were ten thousand men in the Lahgi crater – ten thousand warriors, enacting in symbol the ancient battles of their race, coming hourly closer to the high pitch of dramatic passion that would be vented in the ritual slaughter of a thousand pigs, while the tribes ran wild, trampling the spilt entrails, smearing themselves with blood, screaming and shouting to the climatic fury of the drums.

Against the ten thousand were George Oliver, Père Louis, Lee Curtis and a small handful of Motu police-boys. In other times, in other valleys, it might have been enough. George Oliver had told her more than once of tribal battles stopped and district rebellions crushed by one man's courage and dramatic timing. But now, behind the ten thousand primitives was a twentieth-century man – mad, perhaps, with the explosion of his own pride, but cunning and ruthless, armed with the dark dominion of the sorcerers. A word from him and the chant would turn to a battle-cry and the plumed and painted men would trample down George Oliver and his pitiful army as they trampled the steaming carcasses of the sacrificial swine.

She shivered at the chilling impact of the thought and lay back, drawing the covers about her shoulders. Now she understood the nightmares of George Oliver and her own helplessness against them.

Then another thought came to her. Even at the best, even if George Oliver suppressed the madness, holding it down as a man holds a spring with the flat of his hand and the weight of his bent body, there would still be no triumph in it.

There would still be Kurt. He was her husband in law – and though in law she might free herself from him, she would still be in reach of his malice. Her identity, her new charter of citizenship, was a forgery, at which she herself had connived. The authorities might choose to deport her, not only from the Territory, but from the Commonwealth itself. If they did that, there would be an end of love and of hope, and Kurt Sonderfeld would have the last and the sweetest revenge.

Now it was hers to toss and turn and mutter in her own nightmare, while George Oliver slept peacefully until the dawn was a blaze in the valley and the lizards sunned themselves on the stones and the flaring birds chattered in the casuarina-trees.

Theodore Nelson was in a filthy temper. He had drunk too much and slept too little. His vanity was raw from the repeated snubs of Lee Curtis. He resented the lean, sardonic fellow who sat serenely at the breakfast table after a night of love in another man's bed. While Gerda was in the kitchen, he broached his grievances.

"Oliver, I've got a complaint to make."

"You have?" Oliver's eyebrows went up in quizzical surprise.

"Yes. I asked Curtis for an escort back to Goroka. He refused it. I pointed out that I had obligations to my Company and that the Administration was responsible to the Company for my safety. Curtis was quite rude."

"Was he, indeed?"

"Yes. He called me a coward and a –"

"Well . . . aren't you?"

It was as if Oliver had thrown a glass of cold water in his chubby face. He flushed and spluttered and stammered, while Oliver watched him with cold amusement.

"You – you – I don't have to put up with insults from jacks-in-office. As soon as I get back, I shall make a written report to the Company and to the Administration. I'll see that this business is opened up on – on a ministerial level."

"By all means do," said George Oliver blandly. "I'll make a report, too. I'll point out that when I came last night you were sleeping behind a locked door while Mrs. Sonderfeld was left alone. I'll point out that your Company is one of three competing for the coffee crops in the Highlands and that your representation does little credit to you or to your directors. I'll allege obstruction and disobedience to local authority – and I'll take that one to ministerial level! We're not always one big happy family in the district services, Nelson, but by the living Harry, we close the ranks when a pot-bellied pipsqueak like you starts throwing his weight around! Now, for God's sake, eat your breakfast and stop making a bloody fool of yourself."

Theodore Nelson mumbled vacuously and buried his nose in his fruit. Wee Georgie made a shamefaced entrance at the top of the steps and stood grinning unhappily, just out of Oliver's reach.

"Hullo, boss! Got in late last night, eh? Sorry I wasn't fit to meet you."

George Oliver surveyed him with amused disgust.

"You're a drunken bum, Georgie!"

"I know, boss, I know." He tugged uneasily at his forelock and wished himself a mile away from Oliver's accusing presence.

"Georgie?"

Oliver's voice was poor medicine for a guilty hangover.

"Yes, boss?"

"I'll forgive you last night, because you're shrewd enough to know nothing would have happened anyway. But tonight and tomorrow night, you'll stay with Mrs. Sonderfeld – and you'll stay sober! I'll tell her to cut your ration to half a bottle and keep the key of the cupboard. If you slip this time, I'll have the hide off your back. Understand?"

Wee Georgie nodded, desperately. The A.D.O. was a bad man to cross. He had never been known to break a promise or to make an idle threat.

"I'll lay off it – strike me dead if I won't." He licked his lips fearfully. "You – er – you think there'll be trouble, boss?"

"I'm damned sure there will be. How big it'll come, I can't say. I'm leaving one police-boy here, and I'm posting another at the top of the Lahgi ridge, when we go another into the valley. If anything happens to us, he'll come straight back here and take you and Nelson and Mrs. Sonderfeld south to Goroka."

162

"Gawstrewth!" Wee Georgie swallowed dryly. "So it's like that, is it?"

"Like what, Georgie?"

Gerda stood in the doorway with the breakfast plates in her hand. Oliver made no attempt to reassure her.

He said crisply, "We could have trouble tonight or tomorrow. If a runner comes from me, you get out, fast. You take food and water and a blanket and walking shoes – and you make the best time you can to Goroka. Report to the Commissioner when you get there. Tell him the whole story. Is that clear?"

"Yes."

"That's the girl!" He grinned his approval and pointed to the vacant chair. "Now sit down and let's enjoy our breakfast. I've been long time in the Territory and the worst things that have happened to me have been nightmares and hangovers."

She set the plates on the table and sat down. Wee Georgie squatted on the step and picked his teeth. Theodore Nelson kept his eyes on his plate and ate steadily through his breakfast.

Each for his own reasons was glad of the sardonic reassuring strength of George Oliver.

The cargo-boys were waiting on the lawn. Theodore Nelson sat unhappily on the verandah, smoking a tasteless cigarette. Wee Georgie was shuffling in and out, clearing away the breakfast dishes. Gerda Sonderfeld was in the bedroom with George Oliver.

He buckled on his pistol belt, slung the binocular case over his shoulder, put on his hat and cocked it at a jaunty angle over his shrewd eyes. Then he came to her, put his hands on her white shoulders, and held her a little away from him. His voice was grave and quiet.

"There's something I want to say to you, Gerda."

"Say it George."

"I've told you that I love you and I want to marry you. Nothing can change that."

163

Her eyes filled with tears, but she held them back. She waited while he pieced out his next deliberate words.

"I'm being blunt about it. Nothing would suit me better than to see your husband dead. It would make things easy for both of us."

"I know that."

"But it's my job to bring him back alive, to give him a fair trial and a chance to prove his innocence. I – I propose to do that, if I can."

She tried to move close to him to tell him with her body what her lips refused to say, but he held her firmly away from him and went on.

"I've had a long life in the Service. It hasn't paid me very well; but I've kept my hands clean. I want them clean at the end of this. You understand that?"

"Oh, my dear! Of course."

His eyes softened and his grim mouth relaxed, but still he held her at arm's length.

"It's possible – it's even probable – that I may not succeed. If I have to come back and tell you that your husband it dead, I want you to know, for truth, that I had no part in his death. If you thought otherwise, if you had even the faintest doubt, there would never be any hope for us. You know that."

"I know it," said Gerda softly.

He released her then and saw with a pang of regret that his hands had made red, bruised spots on the white skin of her shoulders. Then she was in his arms, clinging to him, kissing him passionately, and he knew in the instant of wry relief and triumph that she was afraid – not for her husband but for him.

Then he left her and walked out into the sunshine and, as she watched him striding down the path at the head of his tiny troop, she knew that she was seeing the first love and the last hope of all the locust years.

Heedless of Nelson and Wee Georgie and the goggling police-boy, she buried her face in her hands and wept.

164

Late in the afternoon Oliver came to the high ridge of
the crater where Curtis and Père Louis were waiting for
him.

They were camped in a cricle of towering rocks looking southward away from the valley in which the tribes
were assembled. They ate dry rations and slept huddled
together against the cold, lest the smoke of a cooking-fire
betray them to the people in the valley. All day long one
or other of them sat perched between two great tors with
field-glasses trained on the village, watching the ritual
preparations for the great moment of the festival, and in
the evening Père Louis' catechist would come up, furtively, to report on the doings among the sorcerers and
the elders.

When Oliver arrived he went immediately to the
observation post with Curtis and Père Louis and sat a
long time staring through the glasses at the green sweep
of the valley and the sprawling grass huts between the
checker-board squares of the farm patches.

All round the village and along the valley paths white
poles were set up to signify that the pig festival was
near at hand. In the centre of the compound two new
huts had been built – one large and one small.

The larger hut belonged to the fertility spirit. Its
uprights were cut from a sacred tree by a man who held
the office in hereditary right. When the hut was built
and thatched four carvers began to ornament the twin
poles with a crude geometric pattern in which the repeated motif was the long diamond, which represented
the female cleft. They killed a pig to consecrate the
house and hung its fat from the roof-trees as a propitiation to the spirit who gave increase to pigs and gardens
and women.

165

The smaller hut was the dwelling-place of the Red Spirit. It was circular in shape and its centre-pole was a long phallic projection which was kept from festival to festival, buried in a secret place. In front of this hut a large tree had been set up. Its branches had been stripped of leaves and in their place were hung the plumed head-dresses that the men would wear at the festival. It was like a tree full of Birds of Paradise, scarlet and gold and purple and green, fluttering and swaying outside the house of the greatest spirit of all.

The village itself was an eddy of movement and sound and colour.

There was a continual procession of women to and from the garden patches. They came, singing and shouting and gossiping and they returned laden with taro and kau-kau and sugar-cane and clusters of yellow bananas, which were piled in long rows in front of the spirit houses along with the offerings of the visiting tribes.

The unmarried girls were excused from this service. This was the meeting time, the wooing time, which a girl remembered all the years of her married life as the symbol of her lost youth and freedom. Bright with feathers and clattering shell ornaments, girls and youths moved about the village, preening themselves, playing the drums, making kunande in the huts, and love-play wherever there was privacy enough to enjoy the consummation of the erotic rituals.

In the sunlight the wig-makers were putting the final touches on their gaudy confections; while, in the shadowy burial grounds, the sorcerers and the elders held communion with the ancestor spirits on the secret details of the festival.

George Oliver sat a long time watching the threads of colour weave themselves into a primitive but complex harmony – novel to the white man, but older than the panoply that was Solomon's welcome to the dark queen of the south. The oppression of the centuries was heavy on his shoulders and the fear of the centuries' dark secrets fluttered like a bird in his belly. He put down the glasses and set the fuzzy-wuzzy back on watch. Then he turned back to Père Louis and Curtis and jerked his thumb down the slope.

"Let's sit down somewhere. I want to talk to you."

They squatted in the open to catch the last warmth of the sun, for it was late and the shadows were lengthening. Oliver and Curtis lit cigarettes while Père Louis filled his pipe and nursed it carefully to life in the thin mountain air. Then the old man spoke.

"I take it you have been told all that has happened with Sonderfeld?"

Oliver nodded. "Most of it, I think. Where's Sonderfeld now?"

Curtis jerked his thumb vaguely towards the valley.

"Down there somewhere -- we think. We haven't seen him and we don't think anybody else has."

"Would you know if they had?"

Père Louis waved his pipe in a Gallic gesture.

"You must understand that my people are down there also. My catechist came up to report to me last night. He will be here again soon after dark. He says Kumo has been seen conferring with the elders and the other sorcerers. But there is no sign of either Sonderfeld or N'Daria."

"Are you sure he hasn't been killed?"

"Oh, yes. There is still talk of the coming of the Red Spirit. And besides, these people have a sense of theatre. Kumo will wish to stage manage the entrance of the Red Spirit. I believe he will proclaim him at the moment of climax which is at the great slaughter of pigs outside the house of the Red Spirit."

"So, that's where he is !" Oliver snapped his fingers as if at a sudden revelation.

Père Louis shook his head slowly.

"No, my friend . . . no, I do not think so. Sonderfeld is too clever to sit in a cage like a bird waiting for the fowlers. He will be hiding somewhere on the slopes of

167

the valley, in the caves perhaps, or in one of the smaller villages. When all the preparations are made, Kumo will bring him down under cover of darkness."

Curtis broke in, as if anxious to have his own part in the discussion.

"The important thing seems to me to be that Sonderfeld is still master of the situation. According to Père Louis' boy, lots of the ceremonies are being telescoped, while others are being left out altogether, to bring the big ceremony forward. That means Sonderfeld is directing operations and not Kumo."

"He'll continue to direct 'em so long as he holds Kumo's life in his hand."

"He holds it no longer," said Père Louis in smiling triumph.

"What?"

Oliver and Lee Curtis stared at him in gaping amazement. Grinning like a conjuror at a children's party, the old priest held under their noses a small bamboo tube.

"Mrs. Sonderfeld will have told you that she found the brother to this in her husband's pocket."

Oliver nodded.

"That's right. She did. She also told me that you'd given her orders to replace it."

"But what she did not tell you, because she did not know, was that I had removed the contents and substituted another piece of cottonwool, soiled with spittle and blood and tobacco juice to resemble the one I have here."

"We've got him!" said George Oliver with sudden triumph. "We've got him!"

He threw back his head and laughed and laughed till the tears ran down his face. Then he looked up and saw the face of the old priest and the laughter died in him like a match-flame. Père Louis was smiling no longer. His eyes were grave and his old face was lined with fatigue and with sorrow for the follies of the world in which he had lived too long.

"As you say, my friend, we have got him. The power he holds now is an illusion, because we, in our turn, have come into possession of the vital essences of Kumo. It falls to us – you and me – to decide how we shall use it."

"So – so this is what you meant by your stratagem?"

It was Curtis who asked the question. George Oliver was chewing the cud of a new and unpleasant thought.

"That's right, my son. This is my stratagem."

"But – but you said –"

"I said that its use would involve the life or death of a man." He gestured with his pipe. "Ask your superior officer. He will tell you that it is so."

George Oliver looked up and nodded in weary assent. "It's true enough."

"But I don't see –"

"You tell him, Father."

He heaved himself up from the ground and walked a little way down the slope, where he stood backed against the rock looking down into the green emptiness of the valley approach. Père Louis turned his old eyes on the puzzled youth squatting on the ground in front of him.

"To understand what is at stake in this, you must realize that we can do nothing until the great moment of the festival. You could go down now into the valley, you and Oliver and the police-boys. You could demand that Sonderfeld and Kumo be handed over to you. You would be met with blank stares and hostile murmurs, but you would achieve nothing. They would be there. You could beat the valley and still you would not find them – and all the time the people would be laughing at you."

"I know. It's happened to me before in the villages. I've been looking for a man wanted for a tribal killing. I might as well have saved my boot-leather."

"Exactly. So now. . . ." Père Louis took another long draw at his pipe. "So now we are back to the big

169

moment of the festival, the moment when Sonderfeld is revealed as the Red Spirit and proclaimed to the people by Kumo. It is a wild moment, remember. The people are drunk with the slaughter of the pigs, their skins are smeared with blood, the smell of blood is in their nostrils, their memory is full of the old bloody frenzy of the wars. We are there, too. We watch as spectators from the shadows. But we do nothing, because there is nothing to do – nothing at all until the moment of proclamation."

"And then?"

"Then George Oliver – or I, myself – steps forward with this tube and proclaims that Sonderfeld is not the Red Spirit but a liar and an impostor."

"It's one thing to proclaim it," said Curtis dubiously. "The point is, can you prove it to Kumo?"

"That's the least of our worries," said George Oliver bluntly. "The Kiap and the priest – two men who have never lied to the tribes ! We'll convince him all right."

"So !" Père Louis took up his theme. "So, if Kumo is convinced as we hope, he is released from his bondage. No matter that he enters into a new one. He is released from Sonderfeld. What happens then?"

"Then," said Curtis slowly, "then, I think, somebody's going to get killed."

"Exactly," said Père Louis softly. "But who? Kumo or Kurt Sonderfeld?"

"God knows," said Curtis lightly. "I don't see that it matters so very . . ."

Then he saw George Oliver leaning against his rock in an attitude of dejection and utter weariness, and the truth hit him like a smack in the mouth.

"The poor bastard !" he whispered. "The poor, tired bastard."

"I know," said Père Louis softly. "Love is a terrible burden – and the burden of justice is more terrible still."

Shortly after dark, Père Louis' catechist came up to

join them on the ridge. He was sweating with fear and exhaustion and his eyes were rolling in his head. Oliver gave him a cigarette to soothe him, then he squatted in front of them and, in a mixture of pidgin and place-talk, embellished with many gestures, he told them :

Tonight, in the village they were making the prepara-tory magic. Already the first pigs had been taken to the burial ground to be clubbed to death in sacrifice to the ancestor spirits. Their blood would be collected in bamboo tubes and smeared on the house poles and on the lintels of the spirit houses. Tonight the people would eat their meat and feed some of it to the living pigs to fatten them for the great sacrifice.

Then, they would sit in silence round the cook-fires while, inside the spirit huts, the sorcerers played the spirit flutes so that ancestor spirits would hear them and would know that they, too, were invited to the big festival. The women would huddle together and clasp their children close to stifle their crying, and if any of them asked what the flutes were, they would be told that they were the voice of a great bird whose name was Kat, and whose wings they heard beating in the wind and in the storm.

When the flutes stopped playing, there would be a mock battle between the clans. They would shout and stamp and charge each other, stopping in the second before impact. They would rehearse old wrongs and cover each other with insults in memory of the time before the white man came, when there was enmity and killing between the clans.

Then they would sit down together and eat the pig meat and the taro and the kau-kau wrapped in banana leaves and cooked in the ashes of the fire-pits. They would sing together and tell stories and the young ones would make kunande and carry-leg until, at the rising of the moon, the sorcerers would drive everybody into the huts to wait for the coming of the Red Spirit. The flutes would play all night, and on the morrow there would be

171

the great slaughter of the pigs and the Red Spirit would show himself to the people.

When the catechist had finished, Oliver handed him another cigarette and the four of them sat smoking in silence, listening to the small creaking noises of the night and the shuffling murmurs of the police-boys settling themselves to sleep. It was George Oliver who broke the silence.

"When will the great killing be made?"

The catechist swept up his arms in a double quadrant so that they met at the zenith.

"Tomorrow, when the sun is high."

"Day time," Oliver grunted laconically. "That makes it awkward."

"There is a way."

Père Louis took the pipe out of his mouth and pointed eastward along the jagged rim of the crater.

"It means that we rise early and make a half-circuit of the ridge. There is a steep fall into the basin, but if we follow the creek that begins there, we can come down through the jungle and the kunai without being seen."

"How close can we get?"

"A hundred metres perhaps."

"Good enough. Curtis, warn the boys to be ready to move at first light. Then we'll all turn in. Tomorrow's going to be a very busy day."

Lee Curtis nodded and walked over to the police-boys to give them their orders. Père Louis dismissed the catechist with a word and a pat of encouragement and watched him melt quietly back into the shadows. Then he turned to face George Oliver. Oliver held out his hand.

"If you don't mind, Father. I'll take possession of the evidence."

"It's more than evidence, my friend," said Père Louis soberly. "It is a man's life."

"You think I don't know that?"

"I am sure you do. I should like to be equally sure

that you understand your responsibility in the matter."

For a moment it seemed as though Oliver would break into anger, then his mouth relaxed into a rueful grin.

"And what is my responsibility, Father?"

Père Louis shrugged.

"To keep peace among the tribes. To administer justice without fear and with favour to none – not even to yourself."

"Easy to say. But how can one be sure where justice lies?"

"One can never be sure. When in doubt, one is free to accept the most expedient course."

"That doesn't help much, either – afterwards."

"No. Therefore –" Père Louis seemed to hesitate. He bent down and knocked out the dottle of his pipe on the heel of his boot. Then he straightened up. "Therefore, if you wish, I am prepared to keep this – this thing in my possession to do what we both know must be done, and to accept the full responsibility for what comes out of it."

"That makes you the scapegoat for me."

Père Louis smiled a wise, tired old man's smile.

"I am a priest of God. My life is barren of love and my loins are without issue. Why else but to be a scapegoat for my brethren and my friends? It is a little thing, believe me. I am too old to fret and the mercy of God has long arms. Well, my friend?"

"No!" said George Oliver bluntly. "No! I'm grateful, but I can't do it." He held out his hand. "Give it to me, Father."

Without a word, the little priest handed him the bamboo tube that held the life of a man. Oliver looked at it a moment, then thrust it into his pocket.

"Thanks, Father."

The old man's eyes were soft with compassion.

"You are a hard man, George Oliver. Hardest of all, I think, to yourself. I shall pray for you tonight."

173

"Pray for both of us, Father," said George Oliver simply. "Pray for both of us."

CHAPTER 15

DURING the night the sorcerers had been busy. To the sound of the flutes they had danced around the house of the Red Spirit and smeared its posts with pig fat and hung about it the clattering jaw-bones of the slain pigs, so that the people would say that the spirits had eaten of their sacrifice and were pleased with their offering.

Then, from a secret place, they had brought out little boards of casuarina wood, each pierced with a rhomboid hole and daubed with moss. Each of these boards was handed up to a man standing on the roof of the spirit house and slipped over the long, projecting centrepole, in symbol of the act of union. The Red Spirit was the spirit of fertility. Through him the seed quickened and grew to life in the womb of the earth and of pigs and of women.

All through the ceremonies, the sorcerers spoke in the whispered voices of spirit men and the flutes played and the tribes listened, fearful and withdrawn in the smoky darkness of the huts.

Then, when the flutes were silent and even the sorcerers had retired to rest their strength for the great killing, a shadowy figure emerged from a clump of bamboos at the edge of the compound. He wore no ornaments, his face was lowered against recognition and he peered about the deserted compound as if afraid some late-walking lovers might surprise him. But at the sound of the flutes, even the lovers were afraid and they had all gone into the huts to lie in one another's arms until the sunlight came and the evil haunters of the night were blown away with the leaves of the sacred plant which is called bombo.

Satisfied that there was no one watching, the stooping figure signalled with his hand and two others stepped out from the cane clump. They, too, were bowed and naked of ornament, but they carried in their arms the ceremonial wigs and little gourds and coloured pigments and a small bundle of food against the long hours of waiting. They hurried across the compound in the wake of their guide and came to the house of the Red Spirit with its clacking bones and its crown of coital symbols.

The grass curtain was lifted and they climbed inside and drew it close behind them. Then their guide stole another furtive look at the circle of huts and, satisfied that no one had seen him, straightened up and walked swiftly back into the shadows.

Kumo the Sorcerer had accomplished his task. The ransom of his life was almost paid. Tomorrow the Red Spirit would reveal himself to his people.

In the stinking darkness of the spirit house Kurt Sonderfeld and N'Daria lay together in loveless union, and when the first light showed through the chinks of the bamboo wall N'Daria began to daub her master's body with pig fat and paint his face for the moment of revelation to the tribes.

In the village they rose with the sun and purged themselves and began to dress themselves for the festival. Even the married women were absorbed in the unfamiliar rituals of adornment. Some wore coronets of feathers and beetle-shards, but most wore head-dresses of leaves from the sweet-potato vines. Their pubic belts were of fresh twigs and green leaves and their necklets were of green snailshells and crescents of gold-lip trochus.

The bucks and the unmarried girls wore cane belts and Bird of Paradise plumes, while the chiefs and the sorcerers and the ceremonial dancers wore massive wigs of plaited hair, daubed with golden gum and glistening with green beetles and tossing plumes – scarlet and orange and purple and iridescent green.

When they were dressed, the men took up their clubs, whose shafts are made from the wood of the sacred tree, and which are only used for the ritual killing at the pig festival. The women followed them out of the huts into the sunshine, each carrying the family store of taro and kau-kau and bananas, which they arranged in a small mound in front of the spirit house.

Then they squatted on the ground, jostling one another to come as close as possible to the dwelling of the Red Spirit, gasping with wonderment at the sight of the pig bones, nudging one another and pointing at the symbols of fertility that crowned the roof. The children hung about them, chattering, giggling, lost in the wonder of the carnival day, awed by the noise and the colour and the air of tension and expectation. They, too, wore pubic skirts of fresh leaves and the little girls wore on their foreheads or round their necks the diamond of womanhood, so that their breasts would grow and they would mature quickly.

Now the men had withdrawn from the compound, hiding themselves in the bushes and the kunai grass while they donned the last of their finery and finished their face-painting and warmed up the drums for the dance of the Red Spirit, while the sorcerers gave the last instructions on the ritual of the ceremony.

They then formed up – the sorcerers and the chiefs with their great golden wigs, the drummers with their black kundus and behind them the warriors with clubs and spears and stone axes.

Kumo stood in front of them, greatest of the sorcerers, chief paramount of the secret valleys by virtue of his alliance with the Red Spirit himself. His head-dress was a triple tier of Paradise feathers, blue first, then orange and scarlet. His wig hung almost to the nipples of his breast, and two crescent shells hung down from its green fingers. His forehead was green, dappled with yellow, his cheeks were red and his nasal ornaments were a crescent pearlshell and a circle as large as a saucer. Round his neck were ornaments of shell and a stole of possum fur, and in his hand was a great club made of the sacred wood, with a circular head of dark obsidian.

He was a monstrous, challenging figure as he stood surveying the serried ranks of the tribes, holding his stone club high above his head, signalling them to attention, holding them rigid and expectant till his arm swung downward and the drums burst out like thunder and the chant rang round and round the ridges of the valley.

He led them in a wild charge into the compound and through the dancing grove. He dropped to his knees and the whole army followed him. He rose again, shouting, and led them five paces, then dropped again to his knees – three paces, and another genuflection – two paces – one – and they were ranged in front of the spirit house, the drums thudding and the chant going on and on – "Ho-ho-ho-ho" – a surging, wave-like monotony in the still and sunlit air.

Half-way down the steep fall into the valley, George Oliver heard them and looked across at Père Louis. The old priest waved his hand and shouted breathlessly.

"No need to worry, my friend. There is more and more yet."

Oliver raised his hand in acknowledgement and plunged down the slope, stumbling through the thick undergrowth, tripping over trailing vines, stubbing his feet against rocks and fallen tree-boles, until they broke out at last into the tall kunai that masked their last approach to the village.

Cramped and sweating in the half-dark of the spirit house, Kurt Sonderfeld abandoned himself to the mounting fervour of the ritual. The drums were a thunder in his brain and a pulsing fire in his blood. It was as if their energy were being stored up inside him, cramming him to bursting point for the explosive moment of the great revelation. When he peered out through the cracks

177

in the walls, he saw the tossing plumes and the dusty dancing bodies and knew them for his subjects, spending themselves in his honour, preparing themselves by ritual frenzy for the great moment of immolation.

His body was naked, as theirs were. His wig was greater than Kumo's, its plumage richer, its colour a flaring ochre, spilling down over his daubed face and his glistening breast. His arms were bound with cane and golden fur; his anklets whipped like live tails as he walked, and his belt was sewn with alternate rows of gold-lip and cowrie shells. In his hand was the jaw-bone of a monstrous pig.

N'Daria, too, was dressed in her finery as became the bride of the Red Spirit. She squatted on the floor and watched Sonderfeld with doting eyes, all her hurts forgotten, all her fears submerged in the fierce wonder of the drums and the singing and the pounding rhythm of the dance.

Then, suddenly, the drums stopped. The dancers were still. The singers fell silent and there was no sound but the grunting and squealing of pigs, penned in the big palisade.

Kumo raised his club and pointed. Two hundred men went at a run towards the enclosure, leapt the low fence and seized, each one, a pig, looping a halter about its neck and hauling it towards the gate. The gate was opened and a great shout went up as the pigs were dragged out. Then the gate was thrust shut again and the pigs were pulled and pushed into the clear space facing the entrance to the spirit house.

Kumo raised his club again. A group of warriors stepped forward fingering the shafts of their weapons, licking their lips, bracing themselves for the leap. The air was crackling with excitement. Kumo's club swept down in a great arc, cracking the skull of the nearest pig.

A wild cry broke out from the assembly and the warriors leapt in among the pigs, beating them with their clubs, crushing their skulls, breaking their backs, laughing, screaming with delight, splashing in the spilt blood, scooping it up in handfuls and tossing it over the yelling stamping multitude that crowded around the killing place.

When all the pigs were dead, they were dragged in front of the spirit house and stacked in a wide semi-circle, their heads pointing inward to the dwelling of the Red Spirit, their hindquarters splayed outward to the watching crowd.

Then a new batch was brought out and a new batch of warriors made the killings, and the sickening ceremony was repeated time and time again until nearly a thousand carcasses were piled in the compound and the air was full of the stench of blood and the ground was black with flies and the whole crowd was drunk with the smell and the spectacle and the orgiastic delight of cruelty.

Now the great moment was come!

A signal from Kumo and the whole assembly of the tribes were dumb with wonder and expectation. They saw the monstrous figure of the sorcerer mount to the top of the pile of pig bodies and stand there arms outspread in hieratic exaltation. They heard his voice roll over them like a drum-beat.

"Behold, my people! Behold the Red Spirit! Lift up your eyes and see the bringer of riches and the source of all fruitfulness."

There was a moment's pause; then the grass curtain parted and Kurt Sonderfeld stood, deified, on the raised platform of the spirit house, while N'Daria crouched at his feet in an attitude of adoration. For one suspended moment of glory and terror the crowd watched him, his pale body shining in the sun, his head a scarlet wonder, his hands full of promise, his smile a benediction, and a threat.

Then they buried their faces in their hands and moaned – a long, sobbing wail of fear and supplication.

Then George Oliver walked into the centre of the compound.

His voice cracked over them like a lash.

"Fools! Blind fools! Cheated by a liar! Seduced by a coward! They have crammed dust into your mouths and called it food! They have rubbed your faces in filth and called it riches! Lift up your eyes and see! The Red Spirit is a white man, like I am! Kumo the Sorcerer fears him because he holds his blood and seed and spittle in a little tube, like this!"

Slowly, fearfully, they raised their eyes and saw George Oliver standing alone and unarmed in their midst with the bamboo capsule in his hand, and behind him, a long way behind, Père Louis and Lee Curtis with the police-boys, rigid and alert, at their backs.

They looked up at Kumo and saw that he was standing, mouth slack, arms dangling, staring as if at an apparition. Then they looked at Sonderfeld, and as their faces turned to him the big man opened his mouth and screamed at them:

"Kill! Kill! They are liars, all of them! They want to cheat you of the wealth that is yours by right. They are few! You are many! Kill them now!"

But his reason had left him and he spoke in German, which they did not understand and they turned their faces back to Kumo, begging him to interpret for them.

Slowly the sorcerer took possession of himself. He looked at Sonderfeld and remembered the power that lay in his hands. He looked at Oliver and saw that he was unarmed. He looked at his people and saw that they were many and at the police-boys who were so pitifully few. He hefted his club and began to move slowly, cautiously, along the slippery platform of carcasses in the direction of George Oliver.

Oliver stood stock still and watched him come. Then he raised his hand so that the people saw the bamboo tube, and his voice was like the crack of exploding wood.

"Wait!"

Kumo stopped. Oliver paused for two seconds to gather himself for the final attack.

"The white man lied to you, Kumo. He told you he held your life in his little tube. He did once, but not now. I have it. He left it unguarded and I took it into my hands. Look, Kumo – look!"

A long, gasping exhalation went up from the crowd as they saw Oliver stretch out his hand towards the sorcerer. They saw Kumo cringe away, then stiffen as Oliver lifted his voice again.

"I will give you your life, Kumo. I will give it to you now, if you will lay down your club and come to me."

Then Sonderfeld found his voice again. He gave a great shout and leapt towards the sorcerer.

"He lies, you fool! He lies! I hold your life! Look!"

All eyes were turned on him as he stood there, arms outflung, holding in one hand the bamboo tube and in the other the bleached jaw-bone of the great pig. This was the moment of challenge – the moment of choice between the old gods and the new – between the small isolated authority of Oliver and his police-boys and the ancient dominion of the sorcerers.

And the choice was in the hands of Kumo.

He had but to lift his hand in acknowledgement of Sonderfeld and the tribes would rise in fury, trampling down the white men and their alien mercenaries from the coast. Their few weapons would be powerless against ten thousand men and they would be trodden like grass under the black, naked feet. But Kumo hesitated. He was paralysed by doubt. Of the two men who challenged him, Sonderfeld and Oliver, one was a liar and the other had the power to destroy him utterly.

He looked from one to the other. He saw the wild fury of Sonderfeld and the stony calm of Oliver. He remembered that Sonderfeld had once betrayed him through N'Daria and that Oliver was a man who had never spoken a lie to the tribes or made an idle threat.

But it was not enough. His life hung in the balance. He needed more proof. There was none to give it to him.

Then Père Louis stepped forward, small, withered and old, and raised his voice in the tingling silence.

"Look at me, Kumo!"

Kumo shifted his grip on the club and turned slowly to the little priest. Père Louis spoke again.

"Look at me, Kumo, and tell me! Have you ever heard a lie from my mouth? Have I ever taken what was not mine? Have I ever done injury to man, woman or child? Have I not tended your sick and cared for your old?"

He paused. Kumo made no answer. He was tense as an animal at the moment of attack. The old man's voice rose again, vibrant and strong.

"You cannot name me a liar. Hear then when I tell you the truth. The man who holds your life is Kiap Oliver. I gave it myself into his hand. I took it from the house of the red-headed man, whom you call the Red Spirit, and who is a liar and a cheat."

There was a moment of dreadful silence. Kumo turned slowly back to face Sonderfeld. He cried out, desperately demanding an answer from the man whom he had made a god. Sonderfeld opened his mouth to speak, but the words were a frothing babble on his lips. He made wild, flailing gestures but even his limbs would not obey him and the bamboo tube and the bleached bone dropped from his twitching fingers on the bloody carcass at his feet.

N'Daria screamed, leapt from the platform and ran, stumbling and tripping, into the shelter of the bushes.

Then Kumo whirled on Sonderfeld and crashed his club into his skull and, when he fell, struck him again and again, while the tribes watched fascinated and George Oliver stood in helpless horror unarmed in the middle of the compound.

Then he heard Curtis's voice behind him and saw the police-boys coming at a run to seize the sorcerer and

wrench the bloodied club from his hands and hurl him
to the bottom of the small mountain of pigs. They hauled
him to his feet and twisted his arms up behind his back,
and one of them tore off his plumes and his golden wig
and trampled it in the dust, before they ran him stooped
and gasping along the squatting ranks of the women
and forced him to the ground at Oliver's feet.

For a long moment Oliver stood looking down at
him, then he spat contemptuously in the dust and turned
back to face the crowd. He flung out his arms in the
attitude of the tribal orators and his voice rang out sharp
as a sword blade.

"You see what happens to those who turn away from
the white man's law to follow the lying voices of the
sorcerers? You see that the white man is dead and Kumo
too will die in his own time. Your festival is ruined and
the voices of your ancestors will cry out in anger against
you. Their spirits will haunt this valley and there will
come a blight on the crops and a barrenness on your
women. And I, myself, will punish you. I will raise
a double tax on your pigs and on your gardens. I will
set you to build a new road without pay. I will strip
the badges from your luluais and will set new ones to
rule over you. And I will publish your folly to the
Kiaps in Goroka and to the folk in the far valleys so
that your names will be a laughter in the mouths of all
men."

A moan of fear and penitence went up and they hid
their faces from his anger. But they could not escape
the relentless castigation of his voice.

"The festival is finished, do you hear? You will leave
the valley and return to your own homes. When you are
gone, my men will burn this village because the luluai
was a fool who listened to the lying voices. But he will
not depart from it. He will stay here and rebuild it
with his people, because now he is a luluai no longer. Go
now, all of you! Lest you be burnt in the fire of my anger
and die as the white man died – as Kumo, too, will die,

because he killed one man with his club and another by the snake-sorcery."

He turned away from them, but they could not move for the terror of his voice and the anger of the outraged spirits whose festival had been denied them and whose sacrificial pigs would rot in the sun.

Kumo was on his feet now, sullen and glowering, in the strong grasp of the police-boys.

"Take him away," said George Oliver wearily.

"No," said Père Louis. "Not yet."

George Oliver whirled on him. The little priest stood his ground. He held out his hand.

"You owe me a debt, George Oliver. I want it paid."

They faced each other, eye to eye, toe to toe, like wrestlers, looking for an opening. George Oliver was the first to give ground. He fished in his pocket, brought out the bamboo tube and slapped it in the palm of the old man's hand.

"All right, Father, you've got it. Now what?"

The priest said nothing. He stood in front of Kumo holding the tube in his outstretched palm. His voice was low and secret in the place-talk of the tribe.

"Kumo, you were once my son. You are not a fool but an intelligent man. Once you knelt at the altar and received the body of God into your body. Then you turned away to give your soul to the Devil. See now, where he has brought you – to death, which you cannot escape, almost to damnation. See, I hold your life in my hands. I give it back to you, in return for your soul. Turn back to God and I will plead for you with the Kiaps. Even if they will not listen, I will be with you when you die, and I will promise you, in the name of God, the salvation of your soul. Take it, Kumo! Stretch out your hands. Take your life and give me your soul!"

Kumo lifted his head. His eyes were blank. His lips framed the toneless words.

"How can I stretch out my hands when I am held like this?"

184

"Let him go," said Père Louis in Motu.

The police-boys looked inquiringly at George Oliver. He nodded curtly. Kumo was released to stand towering over the little priest. He held out his hand.

"Give me my life."

Père Louis laid the tube in his outstretched palm. Kumo's fingers closed around the tiny cylinder. Then he threw back his head and laughed horribly.

"You offer me my life! You think to buy Kumo, the greatest sorcerer in the valleys! You want my soul? I tell you, you will never have it. Go home, missionary! Go home to your village and talk to the women!"

Once again the old priest's heart sank and his flesh crawled at the spectacle of primitive pride rejecting mercy, rejecting life itself in order to preserve face with the tribe.

He stood there facing the man who had been his son in Christ, wrestling with him for his life and for his soul, praying desperately that Kumo would bend his stubborn spirit to the last mercy. But Kumo was beyond even mercy. In the next instant, he made the act of final rejection.

He raised his hand and sent the tube spinning through the air into one of the smoking fire-pits. Then he laughed again and spat full in the face of the old priest.

Before the police-boys could lay hands on him he had whirled away from them and raced into the thickets. The boys were swift in pursuit, but above the soft padding of their feet, monstrous and horrible came the thudding beat of the taloned claws of the cassowary bird.

Père Louis wiped the spittle from his face and stood waiting while Oliver and Curtis and all the villagers watched him curiously.

He knew better than they the meaning of Kumo's defiant gesture. Locked in the bamboo tube was his life and his life principle – all that primitive man knows of soul. He had tossed away his life. When the fire consumed the bamboo shell, his life would be consumed as surely as if he had been cut down with a stone axe. The old belief was stronger than the new. Its roots plunged down, darkly, to the life-spring itself.

Slow and inexorable, the seconds ticked away. Then, sudden and startling, the bamboo tube exploded in the fire-pit. In the silence of the valley it rang like a gunshot and, before the echoes were dead, from far up the valley, came the long, raucous, soul-wrenching scream of a dying cassowary.

The plumed multitude stood rigid in a long suspension of shock and terror. They rolled their eyes from side to side, looking for one to step forward and lead them out of the cursed valley, away from the vengeful presence of the spirit ancestors and the angry Kiaps, but no one moved.

They saw Père Louis turn away, bowed and shrunken, an old, defeated man, walking slowly out of the village and up the hillside. They saw his few, frightened Christians break from the ranks and straggle after him, like sheep led homeward by a tired shepherd.

Later, they would come to his chapel and confess themselves of adultery and fornication and lapses into the old idolatry, and he would shrive them and comfort them and read them stern lectures on the power of the Evil One and the fate of those who allied themselves with him.

But for Père Louis, himself, there would be neither comfort nor shriving. The nearest brother priest was fifty miles away across the mountains. So he must bear alone the burden of his own presumption. He had tried to bribe a man with the gift of life – which, like the grace of repentance, God holds in His own gift. He had made himself party to an act of despair, a positive rejection of salvation. There was no recourse left to him but mercy, and he felt so old and spent and useless he wondered whether God would take the trouble to bestow it.

George Oliver stood and watched him go, while the

assembly waited, breathless, for his next move. He did not see them. He saw only the figure of the old priest stumbling up his Calvary with the tiny crowd at his back, and his heart went out to him, because he, too, was tired and was beginning to be old.

He had brought peace to the tribes. He had yet to attain it for himself. To the end of his days, he would never know whether he might have prevented the death of Sonderfeld and whether, with prevention in his power, he would have had the courage to avail himself of it. He had tumbled down the idols of the grove, but their shadows were still long across his path.

Then Curtis came and tapped him on the shoulder and said gently, "Go back, sir. Go home and tell her the news. I can handle the rest of it."

George Oliver looked at him a long time before he answered. Then he grinned and held out his hand.

"Good luck, youngster. It's all yours."

Then he, too, turned his face to the hills and began the long trudge back to where Gerda was waiting for him.

Curtis made a sign to one of the police-boys who trotted quietly after Oliver. All the way to the plantation he would walk in his tracks – a faithful servant seeing his master home safely from a long and weary war.

Kumo the Sorcerer was dead on the upland path. N'Daria cowered, lost and trembling, in the bush at the fringe of the camp. Kurt Sonderfeld lay on the mountain of pigs, with the flies crawling over his bloody face.

And, silent among the silent, fearful people, Cadet Patrol Officer Lee Curtis was left alone – master of ten thousand men, fountain of the law, collector of the tribute, lord of life and death in the valley of the tribes.

He was twenty-four years old.

A selection of Bestsellers from Mayflower Books

Novels

EMMANNUELLE	Emmannuelle Arsan	60p	☐
THE FURTHER EXPERIENCES OF EMMANNUELLE	Emmannuelle Arsan	80p	☐
OIL	Jonathan Black	75p	☐
THE WORLD RAPERS	Jonathan Black	75p	☐
THE FOOTBALLER	Derek Dougan	75p	☐
PIPER'S LEAVE	Alexander Fullerton	60p	☐
OTHER MEN'S WIVES	Alexander Fullerton	50p	☐
BURY THE PAST	Alexander Fullerton	50p	☐
THE ESCAPISTS	Alexander Fullerton	50p	☐
THE PUBLISHER	Alexander Fullerton	50p	☐
STORE	Alexander Fullerton	40p	☐
CHIEF EXECUTIVE	Alexander Fullerton	50p	☐
I, A SAILOR	Morgen Holm	60p	☐
I, A PROSTITUTE	Nina Holm	35p	☐
I, A WOMAN	Siv Holm	35p	☐
I, SUSANNE	Susanne Holm	40p	☐
I, A TEENAGER	Tine Holm	40p	☐
KOPTIC COURT	Herbert Kastle	75p	☐
THE WORLD THEY WANTED	Herbert Kastle	75p	☐
LITTLE LOVE	Herbert Kastle	50p	☐
MILLIONAIRES	Herbert Kastle	75p	☐
MIAMI GOLDEN BOY	Herbert Kastle	60p	☐
THE MOVIE MAKER	Herbert Kastle	95p	☐
THE STORY OF SAN MICHELE	Axel Munthe	75p	☐
AMANDA IN SPAIN	George Revelli	50p	☐
AMANDA'S CASTLE	George Revelli	35p	☐
RESORT TO WAR	George Revelli	35p	☐
COMMANDER AMANDA NIGHTINGALE	George Revelli	35p	☐
DOCTOR, NO!	William Rice	50p	☐
DOCTOR, DON'T	William Rice	50p	☐
AN INTERRUPTED FRIENDSHIP	E. L. Voynich	50p	☐
THE GADFLY	E. L. Voynich	40p	☐
THE COAST OF FEAR	Leslie Waller	60p	☐
NUMBER ONE	Leslie Waller	60p	☐
A CHANGE IN THE WIND	Leslie Waller	40p	☐
THE AMERICAN	Leslie Waller	60p	☐
THE FAMILY	Leslie Waller	90p	☐
THE BANKER	Leslie Waller	£1.00	☐

STRAW DOGS	Gordon Williams	60p	☐
THE CAMP	Gordon Williams	35p	☐
THE UPPER PLEASURE GARDEN	Gordon Williams	40p	☐
FROM SCENES LIKE THESE	Gordon Williams	30p	☐
RAMBLING ROSE	Calder Willingham	50p	☐
END AS A MAN	Calder Willingham	50p	☐
GERALDINE BRADSHAW	Calder Willingham	40p	☐
ETERNAL FIRE	Calder Willingham	60p	☐
PROVIDENCE ISLAND	Calder Willingham	75p	☐
REACH TO THE STARS	Calder Willingham	35p	☐
TO EAT A PEACH	Calder Willingham	40p	☐
WANDERERS EASTWARD, WANDERERS WEST (Vol. 1)	Kathleen Winsor	95p	☐
WANDERERS EASTWARD, WANDERERS WEST (Vol. 2)	Kathleen Winsor	95p	☐

Romance

DARK SECRET LOVE	Denise Robins	50p	☐
THE BITTER CORE	Denise Robins	50p	☐
O LOVE! O FIRE!	Denise Robins	40p	☐
FIGS IN FROST	Denise Robins	50p	☐
DANCE IN THE DUST	Denise Robins	50p	☐
BREAKING POINT	Denise Robins	50p	☐
WOMEN WHO SEEK	Denise Robins	50p	☐
AN INTERRUPTED FRIENDSHIP	E. L. Voynich	50p	☐
THE GADFLY	E. L. Voynich	40p	☐
A RAINBOW SUMMER	Emma Woodhouse	40p	☐

War

THE STORIES OF FLYING OFFICER 'X'	H. E. Bates	50p	☐
SOLDIER FROM THE SEA	Alexander Fullerton	50p	☐
A WREN CALLED SMITH	Alexander Fullerton	40p	☐
THE WAITING GAME	Alexander Fullerton	35p	☐
SURFACE!	Alexander Fullerton	35p	☐
THE FREEDOM FIGHTERS	Jean Larteguy	60p	☐
NO PEACE ON EARTH	Jean Larteguy	50p	☐
H.M.S. MARLBOROUGH WILL ENTER HARBOUR	Nicholas Monsarrat	60p	☐
THREE CORVETTES	Nicholas Monsarrat	40p	☐
MOSCOW	Theodor Plievier	60p	☐
STALINGRAD	Theodor Plievier	60p	☐

BERLIN	Theodor Plievier	75p	☐
ALL QUIET ON THE WESTERN FRONT			
	Erich Maria Remarque	50p	☐
WINGED VICTORY	V. M. Yeates	75p	☐

Western

KIOWA	Matt Chisholm	40p	☐
McALLISTER JUSTICE	Matt Chisholm	40p	☐
McALLISTER: THE HANGMAN RIDES			
TALL	Matt Chisholm	40p	☐
McALLISTER: DEATH AT NOON	Matt Chisholm	40p	☐
RAGE OF McALLISTER	Matt Chisholm	40p	☐
THE VENGEANCE OF McALLISTER			
	Matt Chisholm	30p	☐
JUBAL CADE: VENGEANCE HUNT			
	Charles R. Pike	40p	☐
JUBAL CADE: THE KILLING TRAIL			
	Charles R. Pike	35p	☐
JUBAL CADE: DOUBLE CROSS	Charles R. Pike	40p	☐
JUBAL CADE: THE HUNGRY GUN			
	Charles R. Pike	35p	☐
JUBAL CADE: KILLER SILVER	Charles R. Pike	40p	☐
JUBAL CADE: THE BURNING MAN			
	Charles R. Pike	40p	☐
JUBAL CADE: THE GOLDEN DEAD			
	Charles R. Pike	40p	☐

Science Fantasy

THE QUEST OF THE DNA COWBOYS	Mick Farren	60p	☐
THE HOLLOW LANDS	Michael Moorcock	50p	☐
AN ALIEN HEAT	Michael Moorcock	40p	☐
THE JEWEL IN THE SKULL	Michael Moorcock	40p	☐
THE MAD GOD'S AMULET	Michael Moorcock	40p	☐
THE SWORD OF THE DAWN	Michael Moorcock	40p	☐
THE RUNESTAFF	Michael Moorcock	40p	☐
ETERNAL CHAMPION	Michael Moorcock	50p	☐
PHOENIX IN OBSIDIAN	Michael Moorcock	50p	☐
COUNT BRASS	Michael Moorcock	40p	☐
THE CHAMPION OF GARATHORM			
	Michael Moorcock	40p	☐
THE QUEST FOR TANELORN	Michael Moorcock	40p	☐
STEALER OF SOULS	Michael Moorcock	40p	☐
STORMBRINGER	Michael Moorcock	50p	☐
THE SINGING CITADEL	Michael Moorcock	35p	☐
THE KNIGHT OF THE SWORDS			
	Michael Moorcock	50p	☐
THE QUEEN OF THE SWORDS	Michael Moorcock	40p	☐
THE KING OF THE SWORDS	Michael Moorcock	40p	☐
THE BLUE WORLD	Jack Vance	60p	☐
THE PNUME	Jack Vance	50p	☐
THE DIRDIR	Jack Vance	50p	☐
SERVANTS OF THE WANKH	Jack Vance	40p	☐

All these books are available at your local bookshop or newsagent; or can be ordered direct from the publisher. Just tick the titles you want and fill in the form below.

■━━━━━━━━━━━━━━━━━━━━━━━━━━━━━━━━━━

Name_____

Address_____

_____

■━━━━━━━━━━━━━━━━━━━━━━━━━━━━━━━━━━

Write to Mayflower Cash Sales, PO Box 11, Falmouth, Cornwall TR10 9EN. Please enclose remittance to the value of the cover price plus 15p postage and packing for one book plus 5p for each additional copy. Overseas customers please send 20p for first book and 10p for each additional book. *Granada Publishing reserve the right to show new retail prices on covers, which may differ from those previously advertised in the text or elsewhere.*